The Deer Wedding

The Deer Wedding

Penny
Simpson

ALCEMI ✡

First impression: 2010
© Penny Simpson, 2010

Published with the financial support of the Welsh Books Council

Editor: Gwen Davies
Cover: Goldlion

ISBN: 978-0-956012500

Printed on acid-free and partly-recycled paper.
Published by Alcemi and printed and bound in Wales by
Y Lolfa Cyf., Talybont, Ceredigion SY24 5HE
e-mail ylolfa@ylolfa.com
website www.alcemi.eu
tel +44 (0)1970 832 304

for my mother Audrey Ruth

"I believe that love and blistered hands will always build and not destroy."
Ivan Meštrović

"History it appeared could be like the delirium of a madman, at once meaningless and yet charged with a dreadful meaning."
Rebecca West

Contents

Chapter 1 – a suitcase and an Eskimo kiss   11

Chapter 2 – kissing stone   16

Chapter 3 – the wolf and the owls   22

Chapter 4 – the Japanese slug   27

Chapter 5 – fishing for sharks with the Frenchie   32

Chapter 6 – saints and sinners   37

Chapter 7 – coffee with the Pink Panther   41

Chapter 8 – lost & found   48

Chapter 9 – the man in the mask   54

Chapter 10 – Saint Prospero   61

Chapter 11 – grandfather Fisković's saddle   67

Chapter 12 – conversations with Our Lady   73

Chapter 13 – the moth and the fisherman   78

Chapter 14 – Ariel in combats   84

Chapter 15 – eating with bears   91

Chapter 16 – Goran's birthday story   98

Chapter 17 – boat man   103

Chapter 18 – sheep shoes   110

Chapter 19 – jet coat blues   117

Chapter 20 – the heart of the matter   124

Chapter 21 – Elenora's letter   131

Chapter 22 – lemon house   138

Chapter 23 – bard on the beach   145

Chapter 24 – sea wedding   150

On research and inspiration   154

Guide to Pronunciation   156

Acknowledgements   157

Chapter 1
a suitcase and an Eskimo kiss
Zagreb, May 1998

My father died before I was born, so hearing him speak shocks and intrigues me. Zdenka pushes her crazy curls back from her face and looks over. "I didn't know about it, Dagmar. Honestly, I didn't know." She puts her hand on my shoulder and gives me a little shake. "Are you okay?"

No, I want to reply, but I can't. My father's voice is a deep, rich voice, like a proper actor's. He doesn't sound anything like Uncle Darko. I'm listening to him confiding to tape his impressions of a man he interviewed for *Hrvatski Tjednik, Croatian Weekly*, the newspaper that used to employ him. My father says he's met a man who paints dressed in a velvet coat, its lining decorated with little hammers and sickles. He's excited by something he's seen in his studio and then he mentions my mother's name: Ana. He's going to tell her what he's discovered. The loud click of the tape recorder being switched off startles me back into the apartment room where we sit, surrounded by yellowed newspaper cuttings and dozens of cassettes in scratched plastic cases.

"If only I'd checked first," Zdenka says. "How could I be so stupid? But I didn't think for one minute we'd actually hear him."

I've got pins and needles from kneeling so long. I uncurl my legs and touch my toes. Zdenka strokes my back.

"It's not a problem, really it isn't," I try and reassure her.

"I'm an idiot, aren't I?"

"But of course."

We both laugh. Zdenka is, in fact, fiercely intelligent and fiercely determined that other people respect that, particularly the troglodyte males she's surrounded by at university who can't appreciate a woman who thinks for herself – especially not one who wears very high heels, even when travelling on her scooter. Zdenka is a force of nature; she is tall even without her beloved high heels; she's argumentative, stroppy and prone to sarcasm but I love her more than I love anyone else. Maybe because my father killed himself before I was born? Or because my mother abandoned me? Except I'm not supposed to say she abandoned me, because the official line is Ana Petrić went back to her native Ljubljana to re-establish her career. It had been cut short when she was declared a "non-person". My mother occasionally makes her presence felt in my life, either on the end of the telephone, or via a package of *Neu Style* magazines, which she edits.

One day, I'm supposed to make the journey in the opposite direction of those out-of-date magazines. Many years ago, she claimed she would send for me "when the time was right" – or, as Zdenka says – "when she's too old to screw around anymore". Her comments don't hurt me. My mother left Zagreb for Ljubljana shortly before my eighth birthday. The way Zdenka remembers it (and she's six years older than me) she didn't even manage to leave a birthday card behind. Until today, my father has also remained a "non-person" in my life, except when I sneak a look at the few photographs Uncle Darko and Aunty Rozana have kept. I used to have to look at them secretly, because they were hidden away in the sideboard, under old prayer cards addressed to Our Lady.

"I thought there would be more about Elenora in here," Zdenka says, as she stacks up the cassettes. "Maybe an interview with someone who used to work with her at the National, or a recording as Lady Macbeth, or Hedda Gabler. It's amazing what survives, after all."

I'm not going to disagree. Who would think my father would ever come back into my life so dramatically? Zdenka has been distracted again, this time by an envelope of photographs. My father's suitcase is proving a treasure trove for her, at least. It has sat on top of Uncle Darko's wardrobe for nearly thirty years and Zdenka has been hassling him for months to let her open it. She was convinced she would find material for her thesis, because my father researched into the cultural history of Croatia as well as immersing himself in the politics of revolution. She's writing her thesis on Elenora Milković, a long-forgotten actress who once dominated the Croatian stage.

Dazed by what I've just heard on the tape, I don't think I can continue in my role as assistant researcher. I get up to go and buy pastries from Pan-Pek when Zdenka calls me back: "Hey, come and look at this, kiddo." She hands over a rather battered postcard. It's a picture of a fisherwoman painted in oils, but not just any old picture. It's famous, because the original accompanied President Tudman on his historic journey on Vlak Slobode. The Freedom Train was the first train out of Zagreb to the coast after the war ended, and it was felt appropriate to transport "A Portrait of Croatian Womanhood" alongside the President. The painting is by one of the country's greatest artists, Antun Fisković, a native of Split where the train made one of its triumphant stops. From what I can recall from TV reports at the time, Fisković cried off with a bad cold and didn't meet the President.

Zdenka smoothes out the postcard. "I've got an idea, " she says, her brow wrinkled up with concentration. "Let's see." She switches the tape recorder back on, fastforwards it and then stops at random. My father's voice is heard again:

I watch him mix his colours on plain white plates and then carefully spread them over the canvas with the side of his brush, sometimes the tips of his fingers. Fisković works with a concentration you can't break. He has not given up. He has an idea and a desire to realise it. He doesn't settle for second best, or the first attempt. He paints the snow deer over and over again. There is always something new to work in to the frame. We can learn from this. Hope is an entity we can carry from place to place. It's not reliant on an outside force. We in Maspok, the Croatian Spring, also stand on the brink of something new; we stand where Fisković stands each evening, in front of his easel, waiting for the moment to start painting. There can be no compromises with what has been...

I snap the tape off again. It feels too intimate, listening in like this, as if we're sneaking up behind my father, alone in another room, talking to himself and confident he can't be overheard. Zdenka isn't disconcerted at all, but then she's thinking about the woman pictured on the postcard. "This is what we should be writing about, not discredited Party officials. This portrait of a Croatian fisherwoman has meant so much to so many people over the years, but who was she? There's no record of her name, let alone where she came from, or what her life was like. It's the same old story, isn't it? Elenora was silenced too. I

13

mean, I've got a few posters and some reviews, but what does that tell me about the woman herself?"

Zdenka believes the historians of a newly independent Croatia are hopelessly inept at attributing any success for its creation to the actions and lives of women. She is single-handedly going to put that right with her thesis and more besides. Zdenka writes plays and newspaper articles, and she works as an interpreter for United Nations officials who are still arriving in Zagreb to oversee the transition from war to peace.

"Maybe you can make it all up in a play instead?" I suggest.

My cousin wrinkles up her nose.

"I want the details, Dagmar."

I know what she means. I want detail too, detail about Goran Petrić, my father. Who was he really and what was his life like? Uncle Darko and Aunty Rozana have occasionally tried explaining what happened all those years ago, but they usually end up reciting anecdotes that don't say anything important. They remember the brutal outcome of the Maspok rising and my father being forced off *Croatian Weekly* to work as a boilerman in the office basement. And my mother Ana reduced to finding work as a cleaner using a false name, because her own had become a liability after her political talkshows on Radio Zagreb. My father died when he was twenty-four, just a year older than I am now. But what no one ever told me was how beautiful his voice was, nor how much he seems to have enjoyed life and its challenges. The man I've just heard sounds like someone I would like to meet in a bar in Opatovina. He would have views and ideas and we would share Lucky Strikes and Kiwi Cups and I wouldn't feel stupid the way I do when I try and talk to other people, even Josip, my boyfriend.

"You're sure you're okay?"

Zdenka leans over and taps my nose with hers, an Eskimo kiss. *Once, twice and three times for luck.* She's been doing that ever since I can remember. Zdenka taught me to read; later, during the worst days of the war, after Vukovar fell and the President faced calls for his resignation, she started reading out loud to me again. I prayed my mother would send for me and I would no longer be frightened by air raids, but it was Zdenka who ended up taking me to the peace vigils in Jelačić Square. We lit candles as thick as my arm, stamped with the red and white flag of an independent Croatia, and prayed and sang for an end to the bloody massacre that was tearing our world apart. My father should have lived to see such scenes. Had the news that my mother was to have a baby been an influence on him? Did he simply want to escape the responsibility of bringing a new life into a world he despised and that despised him in turn?

Sitting back on her heels (shiny black patent today), Zdenka smiles up at me. She knows best how to win my attention back. "Guess what, kiddo? I'm in love."

My turn to wrinkle up my nose. Zdenka falls in and out of love as fast as a pair of dice spun between a gambler's palms. Her new man is an Englishman called Anthony who works for the UN "in logistics". He rents an apartment off Gradec and owns no fewer than six Paul Smith shirts. Zdenka's eyes shine at the revelation. "I had to move fast," she confides over a Pan-Pek special later. "He's so nice, not like the bloody troglodytes at all. I translated some papers for him and he took me out to lunch. I knew he was the one; in fact, I was so certain, I rang Mile up before we got eating and dumped him, just like that on my mobile!"

Zdenka's laugh is louder than loud. People tend to stop, stare and sigh at the too-tall woman with the too-loud laugh. Zdenka doesn't fit very easily into the world we live in, but that seems to be the way of it with my family. Just look what happened to my father when he challenged the Belgrade communists' stranglehold on his country. I grab Zdenka's arm and hug her to me. Big, brave, brash Zdenka. After Ana left, I asked her if she would like to take on the job of being my mother. We conducted a proper interview, seated on the swings in the little park close to our apartment.

"I'll teach you to spit and beat the losers who want to put you down, and I'll teach you to read and write and be a winner," she promised. "You'll be Princess of the Playground."

And guess what? Cousin Zdenka has kept her word, even when everyone else around us stayed schtumm and fell back on useless platitudes and prayers – and "more damned lies". Zdenka has a big mouth and she paints it in the brightest red lipsticks. She is scared of only one thing: silence.

Chapter 2
kissing stone
Split, May 1932

Antun knew it would work, the minute he caught sight of the block of stone left outside in the courtyard. The sun picked out the sheen of the tiny seashells embedded in the soft cream stone. In his mind's eye, he saw Milan's torso emerge from its nubbly texture, as if he were a storybook's genie softly shooting through a bottle's stem. He crouched down in front of the block and ran his hands over its surface. He could sense by touch alone where his lover's shoulders would break through. He let his hands rest. It was almost a shock to realise it was just stone that he was tracing with his excited fingers. Milan had come alive again as Antun imagined his carving's potential. He looked anxiously around the courtyard, worried he might have been seen so obviously caressing a block of stone. But it was early and no one stirred. He studied the windows in the building opposite, many of them patched over with odd bits of fabric and sheets of cardboard. Several of the tiny windows under the uneven roof were missing frames, or they had been left hanging, their hinges long gone.

He straightened up and lit a cigarette. How to get hold of the stone with Fisković still angry at his sudden return to the workshop the other week? They'd had a huge argument about his leaving college and Fisković hadn't come round yet, not even with Jakob's attempts at intervention. "You might well ask what does a merchant like me know about art? Well, I know this much: what you have is a gift, not just a means to trade."

Antun drew in the smoke from his cigarette deep down into his lungs. Jakob had urged him to return to his studies, conceding only that he should stay home for a few months if he really were that exhausted from his academic labours. But Antun was struggling with something he couldn't really share with his patron, a devout Jew and married man. Quite simply, he couldn't imagine his life without Milan's noisy presence. The workshop in Split, the Academy of Fine Arts in Zagreb, they were just flat backdrops to a life that had come to an abrupt halt when Milan had gone into hiding. He had no idea where he was exactly, but he could make an astute guess. Milan was probably already in Italy, training with Pavelić's Ustaše. And if that were the case, what was the point of sitting in any more life drawing classes?

Antun threw his cigarette down and angrily ground it under his boot's heel. Milan was a fool, but he was also beautiful. Antun had first caught sight of him after paying one dinar for a life drawing class off Ilica, a dismal experience otherwise because it wasn't art that most of the other clientele were after. Antun had been mesmerised at that initial session, just like the voyeurs around him with their empty sketchbooks and blunt pencil stubs. Milan's lean, muscular strength had transferred well into his pen and ink sketches, but later, he found it much harder to convey his extraordinary power with words and the vividness of facial expression. Maybe the stone would finally hold fast his elusive lover? Antun felt tears of frustration prick at the back of his eyes. He could hardly breathe when he thought too long about Milan. He put his cheek against the sun-warmed stone of the wall in front of him, but it felt wrong. The idea that he would never rest his cheek against Milan's flat belly again, nor listen in as his breath slowed after lovemaking was unbearable. He could hardly imagine how he was going to walk into the workshop and pick up his mallet and chisels as if it were just any other Tuesday morning. He wanted to shout his loss out to the cloistered courtyard; he wanted the world to bow down and suffer his grief.

He knew he was being self-dramatizing. It was a fault he'd developed since Milan turned round on his stool and let his robe fall to his ankles; deliberately slowly, his eyes fixed on Antun's. Calculating eyes that had recognised immediately the hunger of desire in Antun's own. Milan knew his worth, measured it out like a pharmacist would a prescription of arsenic. He had taught Antun a hard lesson: it was safe to take a little of what you fancy; take too much, and it would be a living death. Milan had let him take so much because he needed something from him. And that need met, he delighted in paying him back with humiliation and ridicule. But what else could Antun do, but follow his lead? He was in love for the first time – and it would be the only time. He would die, surely, before letting himself experience a love like Milan's again?

Antun returned to the block of stone and walked round it, clockwise and then anti-clockwise. The rhythm consoled him. He remembered his birthday, just weeks ago, running up the stairs to their shared room, Milan several steps ahead, and then Larissa, the pretty girl from the next room along, bumping into them on the landing. Milan's face cruel under the exposed light bulb that lit up their encounter. "You must give Antun his birthday kiss, Larissa. Go on!"

He'd pushed her in the small of her back and she'd knocked up against him, close enough for him to feel her heart beat through her thin chiffon blouse. Antun had flinched visibly when she'd kissed him on the mouth. He'd wiped his lips clean against the back of his sleeve and only then noticed poor Larissa's look of dismay.

Antun tried to blot out the memory. Larissa worked as a secretary in the Sculpture Department, typed up the fees for the models and let him have Milan's address in exchange for a palačinka. His beautiful Milan, living in a room the size of a suitcase with mouse droppings crusted on the floorboards. Milan needed a clean room where he could lie low whenever his political antics brought the police too close on his heels; Antun just needed him. It seemed like a fair exchange at the time, but he had got greedy.

"Hey, you doing a magic trick?"

Antun looked up, startled to find himself back in the courtyard outside Fisković's workshop. It took him a while to identify the speaker, but he found her eventually, on the third floor up, her head poking through a broken window pane. "It's Fisković's boy, isn't it? But you know, I didn't recognise you in that dandy suit. Last time I looked you were a barefoot vagabond."

"I've been away studying."

He tried to remember the woman's name, but failed. She loosened her thin hair from its stringy bun and shook it out. "A likely story, Antun Fisković. You're a born seducer. Just look at you. Enough to tempt a saint."

Antun smiled up at her. He knew her at last, Lidija Vučetić, a whore who worked the little bars off Zagrebačka. Fisković had

18

recommended her when he came of age, whispered her price list to him over a plum brandy and winked in a way that had nearly turned his stomach. But Lidija had shot away inside when she heard Fisković shouting from the workshop. "So, you've decided to stroll in for the afternoon, have you?"

It was barely ten o'clock in the morning, but Fisković would have been up and about since five. Antun knew his routine almost as well as he knew the scars on his hands. He sighed, adjusted his hat and stepped into the workshop. Fisković was sitting on a lump of stone, his hands idle on his lap. Beside him stood two very large, half-finished carvings of angels blowing trumpets. A pot of coffee stood on the windowsill by the door. Antun crossed over and poured himself a cup. The workshop expanded into the next courtyard along, where Fisković carved outdoors under an awning of slatted wood. Inside, he kept his blocks of untreated stone alongside a bench of tools, an old book press and copybooks full of different styles of calligraphy and architectural details. Fisković was a stonemason. His trade was largely the carving of tombstones, but he also helped work on restoration projects in the city. In recent years, that work had been hard to come by, but the steady trickle of deaths in the crowded streets around the Peristyle had begun to make up for the loss.

Antun had worked alongside him ever since he had adopted him as a young boy. Fisković assumed he would inherit the business, but Jakob Eschenasi had had other ideas when he saw his precocious talent. Jakob traded artefacts from across the globe, including ivory carvings from Japan and China, and he knew quality when he saw it. He praised God when he saw Antun had the gift to carve like a Michelangelo and offered to fund his studies in Zagreb. Ivan Meštrović taught there and only he was good enough to channel Antun's latent talent. Meštrović was also renowned for supporting students from impoverished backgrounds. He had been poor himself once; had travelled to Vienna without even a pair of shoes on his feet in order to find an education that would match his talents. Jakob had made contact with the Academy in Zagreb and the sculptor had offered Antun a scholarship on the strength of a single carving depicting a young man in a sailing boat.

Fisković stared over at his son. The old man was nearly sixty and it was showing. The lines on his face looked as though they had been branded. He was frowning into the sunlight that came through the open windows, his brows contracting into a terrible glare. Antun drank his coffee and waited for the storm to erupt. He knew his father's moods only too well. Fisković stayed surprisingly silent.

"I went for a walk," Antun began. "I went up to the chapel in the Marjan Hill. I wanted some peace and quiet."

"Barely turned twenty and you're planning to die, are you?"

"No. I just wanted to see the sun come up."

"Ah, you watch the weather, and I work myself into a grave. That's the plan, is it?"

"Pappa, I'm sorry. I'll stay on tonight. We'll get everything finished."

"It's not the commissions I'm worried about. It's you. Moping like a bloody girl." Fisković paused. A sly look came over his face, rather similar to the one he had adopted when he'd talked up Lidija's charms. "Your mother thinks it's a girl, anyway."

Antun found himself blushing. He quickly turned to look out of the window. "I'm not sure about my college course, that's all."

"And I'm sure you have the brain of a grasshopper," Fisković thundered back. "One minute here, the next minute there. Make up your mind, once and for all."

Fisković lurched off the stone block and headed back out to the courtyard. Minutes later, Antun heard mallet strike against chisel, a sound as familiar to him as the summer cicadas in the hills beyond. He put his cup down and went over to inspect the angels. Fisković was experimenting with a new pattern and he'd struggled to carve a trumpet without disaster. Antun ran his fingers over the hands of one angel. They were still a rough sketch. He knew Fisković was waiting for him to take up his chisel and smooth away the planes, because he was more likely to finish such a task without mishap. At the feet of the angels, several chipped fingers sat like a warning. Antun turned one of the fingers round between his own. His father didn't seem to consider that there were times when a piece of stone had to be tempted to give up its secrets, cajoled like a small, shy creature. Stone might seem solid, but Antun had always relished the challenge of making it respond to his touch, like a lover under his palms; stroking and easing skin and bone; teasing out the details, melding insight and technique until the secret inside the stone emerged. He looked up and found himself eye-to-eye with one of the angels. She was boss-eyed. "Damn, I'll need to start the whole thing from scratch," he thought. "That's why Pappa is so angry."

Chapter 3
the wolf and the owls
Zagreb, May 1998

The owl family is still in place, a little dilapidated and stowed away under a wire mesh, but otherwise unharmed. It was one of the last things I remember seeing, before taking a train out of Zagreb – forever, or so I thought. Sometimes, it feels as though I left in another century, but actually it was only fifteen years ago. I try and convince myself that the survival of the owl family on an apartment block near the station is a good omen, but my rising sense of panic is getting the better of me.

"Can you stop?" I ask the cab driver.

He shrugs, but parks up, close to the National Theatre. I stumble out and wait for my feelings of panic to pass. Deep breaths. In and out, in and out. I try and distract myself by watching what else is going on around me. A woman is weeding the flower beds opposite the theatre; chairs are being set up outside cafés and the felt grass squares in front of them are being slowly swept of fallen leaves and abandoned cigarette packets. A tiny, blonde-haired girl walks a huge dog on a lead. It's as if I've never been away. I almost expect to hear Goran calling me from the cab. "You okay, Ana? Shall we go back to the apartment?"

But our apartment disappeared long ago, and not long after that Goran went too. I had to leave, because I was lost in this city without him. And now? I'm back because I've been asked to conduct an interview with President Tudman, live on Croatian TV. I'm back, because I'm a survivor like him. "A fellow traveller," he called me in his letter. It must be the only reason I return. Everything else is lost to me. I don't expect anything else to happen, but my panic attacks and sleeplessness give the game away. The truth is, I really do want to see them, Darko, Rozana and my little girl. Except she's a grown woman now – twenty-three on her last birthday. I sent her a beautiful bronze scarf, hand embroidered with a feather fringe, the gift of a Slovenian designer I'd profiled in *Neu Style*. I have no idea if it was the right choice.

"Bloody wolf, not a dog," says the cab driver, nodding to the little girl and her pet, as I return to the car.

He holds the door open for me, sensing I'm someone with a history he should maybe acknowledge, but I don't think he recognises me. He can't have been much more than a schoolboy when I first took to the airwaves of Radio Zagreb. He's maybe thirty, a chain smoker and garrulous. His face is flat like a sting ray's and he has very hairy, muscular shoulders visible beneath his vest. Maybe he's been serving in the army, or with the paramilitaries? We start a conversation about the hotel I'm booked into, just off Ilica. His cousin helped build the place, one of many being constructed to meet demand.

"UN bureaucrats, not tourists," he says, but without rancour. My cab driver has evidently made a pretty profit from the overseas peacekeepers and their administrators, judging by his designer sunglasses and exquisite Armani black jeans. "And you're back for pleasure, of course," he says, studying me without embarrassment in his mirror. "Are you from the city?"

"Once upon a time, not anymore."

"Ah, the story of our times."

He swings a sharp left, across a tramline, and we're outside Hotel Callas. He jumps out and delivers my suitcases to the reception lobby before taking his farewell. He kisses the back of my hand and declares he knew me at once. "My girlfriend watches all the soaps," he confides. In some ways, he's right. I am an actress, although I suspect a poor one. The receptionist waves him away and checks my reservation details and passport.

"Welcome to Zagreb, Mrs Dodig."

"It's Ms Petrić now."

She shoots me a look, but doesn't comment. My room is the first off the corridor leading from the breakfast verandah. It's compact, not luxurious, but what I expected after my conversation with the cab driver. I don't take long to unpack, but spend some time checking my emails. I had hoped my visit wouldn't compromise deadlines for the next issue of *Neu Style*, but everything has been thrown upside down by the collapse of our cover feature. I fire back a suggestion that I work up my interview with the President, but I doubt we can persuade him to model the same suits we planned for the Slovene actor and award-winning skier Ivo Kucar. Besides, rumour has it the President has not made progress after surgery for stomach cancer. The interview might yet prove to be a phantom.

Back at reception, I ask for a map. I've seen the television news reports about the air raids in Zagreb and haven't been sure what to expect. Outside in the streets, all looks much as it did before, except people look less drab. The fashions are current, the young men and women walking in Gornji Grad all cut from the same pattern: tall as catwalk models and just as striking. I dread catching their eye: what if one of them turns out to be Dagmar? When I've imagined our first meeting, I never thought of it taking place impromptu on a street corner. Since I booked my trip, I have built up the idea of our reunion into a Chekhovian-style scene, acted out in Rozana's front room – but hopefully without that awful draylon sofa and giant sputnik table lamp to distract from the emotion of the moment.

My daughter. It sounds odd, even whispered to myself. Can you still claim to be a mother when you've rarely seen your child outside of a photograph, when you've never held her after her nightmares, or wiped her tears, or cheered her on in a relay race? What I have done is live a lie. I'm not a mother. But each step back to Jesuit Square convinces me I do have a claim on the title. I left, I know, because I needed to give myself a chance, one I could never have been given in the old Croatia, "the silent republic," which had destroyed a whole generation. My generation. I think of the song by The Who, one of Goran's favourites. He'd played it at top volume on Darko's record player before we went to the rallies, ignoring the angry shouts of the neighbours below. We'd screamed ourselves hoarse, demanding change, a new constitution free of Belgrade's control – and, most passionately of all, a future. But our brave roar had been reduced to that deafening silence.

I head for St Katarina's, the church in Jesuit Square I attended when I still lived here. It's hard to think why a church should be my first port of call, as it was the church that turned its back on me as squarely as my former employers had at Radio Zagreb. Goran had committed a sin when he took his life, according to my church's teachings. Another door closed, and my heart had broken. But still I can't resist a look. The young woman I had once been loved the ceremony and mysteries of the Mass; once I'd even thought of becoming a picture restorer so I could spend my life rescuing old church frescoes and involving myself in a non-stop Mystery Play, acted out by centuries-old figures missing eyes, limbs or jewelled headdresses.

Inside, it takes a while for my eyes to acclimatize to the shrouded gloom. I hunt out the side chapel where the Virgin stands, fairy lights twinkling above her head and plastic ivy twined around her bare feet. Small bouquets are slotted in the rail around her shrine, some carrying little prayer cards. I cross myself and kneel down. Shortly afterwards, an old woman joins me, dropping two heavy shopping bags either side of her. The church has always been a favourite for the housewives on their way home from Dolac market. The woman prays fervently under her breath. Suddenly, the church springs into a blaze of colour and movement. Someone has put on the overhead lights so that a party of tourists can record the interior on their camcorders and the church is revealed as a baroque interior of amazing splendour – every square inch decorated with dancing putti, framed by pink and white garlands. I sit quietly, as always stunned by this view. I have no words to offer Our Lady, so light a votive candle instead.

Leaving the church, I walk into the nearest café and order a black coffee and a Jamnica mineral water. I don't need a map to take me to Darko and Rozana's apartment, but an armed escort to stop me running when I approach the entrance. What are my feelings about returning to my old home? Guilt, apprehension and despair. I have left it too long, I know. But what is strange is how it doesn't feel like fifteen years have gone by; one minute, I was a young woman desperate to escape a world that had stripped me of my identity for a crime I didn't understand. The next minute, I'm here sitting in this café, sipping coffee like any other elegant, middle-aged divorcee, my past a footnote in a text book (if that) and my immediate concern writing a list of questions for Croatia's esteemed President. The Maspok survivor; the people's hero. Who would have thought it, after what has been?

Goran wanted independence for Croatia, like Tudman, but would he have been happy paying the price that was eventually paid?

Goran has disappeared into the past, like the dancing putti into the gloom of the unlit cathedral behind me. He's a shadow, not a real life person. Defeat left him vulnerable; he barely spoke to me during the last few months of his life, caged up in his brother's apartment like a sacrificial ram. In the end, he'd delivered the blow himself. I've never forgiven him for leaving me behind. Is this what I'm afraid to tell my daughter? I can't remember your father, not the flesh and blood man, just the shadow who silently exited my world, softly like a stone dropping through an ocean. For she will ask me things I can't hope to answer, I know that. She will ask the questions I asked myself in the days before I found my new life. She is twenty-three, with all the resolve and conviction of anyone else her age, the same formidable confidence of being right which I once possessed when I questioned Yugoslavia's government ministers relentlessly on my radio show. *Behind the story with Ana Petrić.* But the one story I should have held on to and explained has been deleted by time and Goran's final act of despair. Dagmar would hate such a spirit of defeat, if she's anything like I was in those days of protest.

Maybe I can turn the tables. I can ask her questions, because I'm the master interviewer when all is said and done. I take my mobile out of my handbag and check down the list of names. And there it is: Darko's number. 796-046. I'm about to ring when the waiter glides up and asks if I want anything else. The moment is lost.

Chapter 4
the Japanese slug
Zagreb, May 1998

I'm on the early shift at Mimara, so pick up my breakfast at Dolac market. At this time of day, everything has just come in from the countryside and still looks fresh and vivid. There are piles of pale-skinned peppers lined up alongside barrels of multi-coloured beans: twists of herbs, apricots, peaches and huge slices of watermelon. I buy apricots and peaches, wrapping them in a shawl in my rucksack to stop them from bruising.

The steps leading down to Jelačić Square have already been commandeered by the flower sellers who sport a rich variety of patterned headscarves. Some of them recognise me and call out greetings, because I often buy a spray of flowers for the staff room. Close to the square, there's usually a tiny old woman in position, holding out her arms, each one adorned with dozens of pairs of black and cream lace gloves, all the way to the crook of each elbow. Her fingers are twisted and gnarled like a tangle of roots and I wonder how long it must take to make her beautiful gloves. Surely you'd need fingers swift as butterfly wings to weave them into such fine patterns? I call her the Black Widow, because she always dresses in black from head to foot; black headscarf, cardigan, skirt, apron and a man's pair of black, lace-up shoes. They look far too large for her doll's feet, as if she has put on her husband's shoes by mistake. She never looks at passers by, just holds out her trembling arms and waits for someone to stop. She looks so terribly sad I don't suppose anyone would dare walk away without buying something.

Today, there is a crocodile of Japanese tourists who are filming the flower sellers and the Black Widow on tiny camcorders. I wriggle past and out onto the square. A traffic cop in a white baseball hat holds up his lollipop-shaped baton to let me cross into Ilica. It's nearly summer. I'm hungry already and stop to buy grilled corn on the cob at the little stall off Frankopanska. I eat it on a bench sat outside Mimara, watching rollerbladers practising their moves round the flowerbeds. Several of the boys wear football shirts, each embroidered with Bilić's name. Our new national hero after our World Cup success. The salt on the cob grits my lips. I clean up with a tissue and check my watch.

Ten minutes left before I need to sign in. I sit back, close my eyes and let the morning sunshine wash over me. It's a morning just like any other, except everything is tinged by yesterday's discovery. I can still hear my father's voice when I stop and concentrate. Inside my rucksack, I have an old Walkman of Zdenka's and one of the cassette tapes we found in Uncle Darko's suitcase. If it's quiet today on my watch, I'll sneak a chance to listen to it. I should have time to memorise the entire tape, except Josip keeps interrupting me. He's also working at Mimara. He likes the quiet and the stillness more than I do, largely because he can test out his drumming skills on top of the windowsills.

Josip is a drummer in a band. He has dyed blond hair and a goatee beard. We met on a training course run by the gallery and bonded over our shared liking for a Japanese casket from the Edo period. The eighteenth-century casket opens up to reveal two tiny drawers, each one decorated with a riot of enamel detail. All insect life is to be found in its design: a spider, a dragonfly, a beetle, a ladybird (its spots picked out in rich jewel colours) – and a slug.

"There are slugs in Japan?" Josip had asked the curator leading the training session.

The curator had struggled to reply.

Josip is interested in the obscure details of the world around him, because he uses them as references for his songwriting. *Slug From Japan* was one of his first efforts, its rhythms thrashed out on a windowsill with his index fingers one slow, summer afternoon. Josip and his band are drawn to the irrational, the surreal – and to anything that originates from their internet contacts in Slovenia and beyond. They are "proto-punks". This means their disgust at the actions condoned by our political and military leaders during the war is refracted through juxtapositions of real facts and weird imaginings. Zdenka thinks they're puerile hypocrites who avoid engagement with the real world because they just want to become rock stars and live abroad.

"And how is that going to make a nation proud of itself?" she demanded one night in De-Stress, the nightclub in Gornji Grad where Josip and his band play on Friday nights. "It's all swagger and no substance."

Even the name of Josip's band can't stay the same for two days running. There are regular disputes between the players over the right name and image to project. It's not unknown for two different factions of the same band to compete for the same slot on the same evening in De-Stress, a competition which has led to fights, arrests and a very dramatic scar on Josip's left cheek. He's convinced he's an anti-hero second to none (and certainly not inferior to Dunk, the bass player). Josip currently claims the band is called Brain Drain. Dunk contradicts him and says they've been Mohican Riot since at least April. This morning, he's in a vile mood because Dunk has fly-posted a gig he's not agreed too – and put Mohican Riot on the posters. "It's out of order. We're all supposed to be equals."

"But you made up Brain Drain on your own."

"It went to a vote."

"Dunk said it didn't."

"He was wired, so he can't remember voting."

Josip slips down the wall beside my chair and rests his head on my lap. He's humming something and I hope he doesn't ask me my opinion. If it's one of his songs and I don't recognise it, I'll be in deep shit.

"What are you listening to, Dagmar?"

He's spotted the tape player in my jacket pocket, slung on the back of the chair.

"Nothing."

"Bet it's Blondie." He puts the headphones on and listens in, but only for a few seconds. "What's this bastard going on about? Haven't you got the demo we did at De-Stress last month?" He throws the player into my lap. "Can't you even pretend to show an interest anymore?"

"It's my father, if you must know."

"What is?"

"The voice on the tape."

29

Josip stares back at me. I've not told him much about my parents, except that my father died before I was born. Today, he's too self-obsessed to try and accommodate my concerns. I know that, so I should just change the subject and be done with it, but I can't stop myself. It suddenly seems very important that Goran Petrić isn't dismissed all over again.

"We found some tapes my father made when he was a journalist. Back in the Seventies." I pause and Josip shifts on the floor at my feet. He's uncomfortable with the conversation, but I push on. "My father was a Maspok martyr. Do you know what that means?" Josip nods. He doesn't look me in the eye. "My father was a non-person. But now he's someone again. I've heard him, and I want to know him better."

"But he's – "

"Dead. Yes, I know. But there are people still alive who knew him. There are more tapes. There are letters, notebooks."

I've started crying, which makes Josip even more edgy. A visitor has walked into the gallery from the far side of the room. I still can't stop crying. Josip leans over and whispers: "Shut it, Dagmar. There's somebody else here now."

I get up from my chair and run out of the gallery. I keep on running until I'm back outside, sitting on the bench where I started this morning. It's close on lunchtime and the heat of the day has started to build. I'm still crying. One of the rollerbladers shoots to a halt in front of me.

"Hey, lady. You'll make yourself all ugly." He plucks a flower from the nearest flowerbed and tucks it behind my ear. "Whoever he is, he's stupid. Come for a drink with me instead?"

I wipe my eyes with my sleeve and shake my head. He strokes my hair. That gives me courage to finally ask the question I wanted to ask Josip back in the gallery. "Is there any point in bringing the dead back into your life?"

The boy in front of me is what, sixteen, seventeen? Too young to have fought, but not too young to have lost someone, maybe a father or a brother. He understands full well I'm talking about the war. He's embarrassed, because it's what we all think about, but in public, spoken out loud, the story has to be told differently. He shrugs his shoulders and scoots off to re-join his friends. Someone else has sat down beside me

30

in the meantime, a man I think is one of the gallery managers, although I don't know his title. He has the beauty of a Roman carving, and the easy assurance of the blaggers I've met in Ilica on close, summer nights. He's wearing a loose linen shirt, skinny jeans and a pair of beautiful leather loafers. A man as proud as an eagle, and probably with cause.

"The past is a dangerous place, is it not?" he says, but it's not really a question. He introduces himself as Marko Strgar. He's a curator at the gallery, he adds, currently working on a large-scale retrospective that is planned for early next year. "I've been campaigning for this exhibition, which is dangerous in its own way, because of its subject matter. It is, I suppose, about the past as much as it's about anything."

"What kind of exhibition is it?"

I'm curious about this man, whose self-assured behaviour reminds me of an actor delivering a piece of highly polished performance art.

"It's the first retrospective for Antun Fisković to be staged in Croatia – or anywhere else, come to that. His entire oeuvre – sculptures, drawings, paintings, even the doodles on his shopping lists. It feels like *my* life's work putting *his* life's work into perspective."

The coincidence of it being Fisković's retrospective startles me. I want to ask more, but Strgar has to take a call on his mobile. Later, walking back through Dolac market, I wonder if I might find out more about my father's investigations through talking with Strgar. Listening to the tapes, I realise my father was planning to write about Fisković, but something stopped him. There had been a discovery in his studio, one he had wanted to share with my mother, but then nothing more was said on tape and my father never wrote his proposed article. I mention Strgar to Zdenka when I get back to the apartment. She's excited too, but that's because she's found out Fisković was a student of Ivan Meštrović and Meštrović had employed Elenora to model for his life drawing classes.

"Everyone always knows everyone in a place like Zagreb," she enthuses. "And think about it: Fisković might have been at those classes. He might have drawn Elenora. I need to meet this Strgar and see what's being included in this show of his."

Chapter 5
fishing for sharks with the Frenchie
Split, May 1934

The shoreline in the early hours of morning was no place to find solitude, but its busy detail had long inspired some of Antun's best sketches. This was where the fishermen from neighbouring islands came to trade, turning over their boats and improvising a market down by the water's edge. The fishermen caught up on news as they worked, shouting across the upturned hulls or meandered between each other's catches, a clutch of fish hanging from their belts on a piece of twine. Sometimes, they brought their women over to gut fish, as the prices rose and fell around them. These were strong, boisterous women with skin raw from biting winds. They tucked oil cloths round their full black skirts and wrapped their heads in heavily embroidered scarves before lifting the baskets of fish to rest there, balancing carefully as they did so in the bloody guts at their feet. Antun liked drawing the curves of the women's wooden clogs matched by their bare arms, sunk to the elbows in barrels of salted fish.

It was summer, and the stink of the catch was almost beyond endurance. Antun worked at his sketchbook with a scarf tied across the lower half of his face. He drew the women as they swept their baskets up onto their heads, the arc of their arms caught in thick charcoal strokes. He was engrossed in his work and didn't hear his name being called. It was only when someone gently stopped his hand that he looked up and discovered Jakob. Antun shifted along the wall to make room for his neighbour and friend.

There had long been a rumour claiming Antun had been rescued from a shipwreck and brought to Jakob's warehouse. The merchant had standing amongst the locals and few doubted that he would have been the best authority to deal with an orphan washed up by the sea. Jakob had taken the boy to the Fiskovićs, a childless couple who lived close by his warehouse in Split, and they had adopted him. This was the story that Jakob told Antun when he was six years old, sat in his adopted father's workshop on top of a pillar, his heels kicking against its marble contours. He wasn't the son of a mermaid, after all, but that of a poor, young actress who had not been able to marry his father. Jakob had stayed part of his life, always displaying an eager interest in his progress. It was the thought that Jakob was paying for his studies that stopped Antun's tongue.

Jakob was a tall man with an imposing bearing. He wore beautifully tailored robes and small, embroidered skullcaps that were the envy of the fisherwomen. He had a heavy, low brow and an impressive aquiline nose, but it was his lips that caught the eye, as defined as a Roman statue's and a startling pink like a young girl's. Antun waited for him to speak. He felt he was letting Jakob down, even more than he was his father.

"So, I find you drawing." Jakob turned and smiled. "This is appropriate. You must never stop drawing."

"I don't plan to."

"Only to stop studying?"

Antun set down his sketchbook. He wished he could explain to Jakob the grief that had led him to run away from Zagreb.

"I wrote to Meštrović last night," Jakob continued, completely unaware of Antun's predicament. "I have asked him to consider taking you back in the autumn. All is not lost." Antun could only disagree, so he stayed silent. "I know you're not a hothead. A talent like yours stands beyond the ebb and flow of man's more temporal desires. I hear they plant bombs in Zagreb."

"There are some extremists, but most stick to arguing in the cafés."

"And you, Antun. Have you maybe argued with someone and found yourself in trouble? It happens when politics mixes with too much plum brandy."

"I don't really know about politics. I just draw."

"A wise man knows when he must speak out."

"I get laughed at when I speak, Jakob."

"Why is that?"

"Because of my accent and because I can't speak Hungarian or

German. And I'm a Dalmatian, which is worst of all. A Dalmatian who puts too much pepper on everything."

Jakob laughed and patted Antun's arm, but his tone was serious when he replied. "You should never be ashamed of where you come from, or who you are. Your heritage is a rich and splendid one. I'm a Jew and I have traditions that single me out too, but I take pride in that and ignore the narrow minded. Sadly, they are often the ones who shout the loudest, but that's because they have fear in their hearts. What else do they have to prove they are alive? Just their prejudices that can turn on them, like wolves."

Antun stared down at the fishermen's boats. He knew in essence his patron was right, but it was hard to act on his words. He recalled Milan's angry outbursts, late at night as they lay together on his narrow truckle bed. Milan was always listing his enemies, an endless roll call that took in everyone from the Government in Belgrade – all scheming bastards with bottomless pockets for bribes – to the poor caretaker at the Institute, a one-legged Serb married to a Croatian. They had six children, a fact which had appalled Milan. "Six, yes, no fewer than *six* impure vermin," he had raved, beating his fist on Antun's naked chest, one blow for each unfortunate child. "How long must we put up with the infiltration of our race? We must have our freedom and the Serbs must go and live in Serbia. They are not wanted here."

He had fallen back on his pillow, exhausted by anger, and not, much to Antun's annoyance, from bringing him to a crazed climax. Politics had crept between them over the months, ensuring fewer and fewer moments of physical contact. Antun felt rejected. He had pleaded like a woman for sex, and Milan had shown his disgust by beating him. The memories of the blows made him blush. Jakob didn't notice anything untoward, just waved at someone he saw coming down the Promenade. Antun's eyes had filled with tears, so he didn't recognise the figure in the far distance until she came closer. It was Tilde, Jakob's daughter, a twelve-year-old sprite in an outfit of her own devising. Jakob adored his only child, allowed her the run of his warehouse and its marvels, and she took full advantage. Today, she wore a linen coat embellished with buttons covered in tiny shards of sparkling glass and a straw hat, secured to her head by a thin strip of gauzy fabric, decorated with bright gold sequins.

"Have you stepped out of an Arabian Night?" Jakob asked, proud of his maverick child.

Antun recovered his composure and found enough courage to begin a conversation with the lively Tilde. She could hunt out a secret like a dog did a truffle.

"Will you draw me, please?" she asked, snatching at his charcoals and pretending to hide them behind her back.

"You're too beautiful. All my other clients will be jealous."

"Liar!"

Jakob shook a warning finger, but Tilde ignored him. He might make the rules, but she chose which ones she obeyed. She sat down beside her father and rested her chin on his shoulder. "Pappa, can we buy fish today?"

"Of course. What sort do you want?"

"I want to eat a shark. A whole one."

Jakob pulled out an old leather wallet and made as if to search for a handful of coins. Antun didn't see how the joke played out, because he had finally caught sight of the one person he had hoped to see all that morning. He was the fisherman known as the Frenchie, because he had once found a Napoleonic coin in Hvar's fort. His real name was Branko Ostojić. He was everything Jakob had implied a true Dalmatian should be: a proud, self-possessed man dressed in a traditional loose linen shirt, breeches and soft leather boots. He had known Branko forever, fished with him as a boy and visited his family's home on the island of Hvar many times. They had carved their wrists with his fishing knife and let their blood flow as one. Blood brothers. Antun smiled with genuine pleasure as Branko strode up to them and offered his greetings. His hair, bleached in the sun, fell into his eyes. For a short while Antun stared at him, but then Branko tugged his hair away from his forehead to reveal a fresh wound. "Fell, didn't I, just as we landed the first catch last night. Cut myself with my own knife."

Tilde squealed. "Was there lots of blood, Branko?"

"Enough for you to bathe in, little one."

She squealed again. Branko took her hand and she sang to him as they walked towards his boat. "Buy me a shark, a lark of a shark, for my tea-o."

Jakob turned to Antun. "Such an imagination. It frightens me, to tell you the truth."

Antun wanted to reply that it wasn't a person's imagination that was ever at fault, just the things that happened to them. Besides, a strong imagination was just about the only thing that was keeping him sane. He put away his sketching things and jumped down from the harbour wall. He would buy his fish from Branko and maybe, if he felt really brave, he would ask if he could join him and the other fishermen out drinking that evening.

Chapter 6
saints and sinners
Zagreb, May 1998

I didn't expect Dagmar to open the door. I look at the young woman
and try and match her up with the child I left behind all those years
ago. She's shorter than me, a lot thinner, with cropped bleached hair
and beautiful green eyes. My professional instinct picks up on the
lovely pale skin and the distinctive dress sense: a military jacket worn
over a tutu skirt and leggings. Her feet are bare and she's wearing black
nail varnish. My daughter. I want to acknowledge this to the whole
apartment block, but I can't even find words to explain what I'm doing
on the doorstep. She smiles, hesitantly. "Can I help you?"

She doesn't recognise me, but why would she? I expect Rozana
has eaten all my old photographs. This momentary spite helps cover
my sense of shock, no, my pleasure at meeting such a wonderful
individual. Is this evidence of maternal pride, or am I just saluting a
young woman with style? Inside the apartment, people are talking and
laughing. The Petrićs have company. I wonder whether it might be
best to try another day, but someone else has walked into the hallway.
Dagmar is suddenly pushed away from the half-open door and there
stands my former brother-in-law. Darko has grown older, that's for
sure. Worry lines mark his brow and his hair has thinned and receded.
He used to have thick, curly dark hair, like a Roma boy.

"My God, it's not possible."

He blocks the doorway, but Dagmar is determined to find out what
is going on. She pops up under his arm, which is tightly gripping the
doorframe.

"Who is it?" she asks, still smiling. She's not picked up on the
tension, but is staring at my shoes, red crocodile with silver heels.
"They're great."

Darko is flustered.

"Now is not a good time," he attempts to explain, but he's
interrupted in turn by another woman's voice, calling from the kitchen.

"Don't keep people standing outside. Bring them in." The woman who has just spoken comes into view. It's Rozana. She makes the sign of the cross when she sees me, as if I were a devil or a vampire. Dagmar is irritated that no one has introduced me. It doesn't take her long to work it out however, after Rozana's gesture.

"Yes," I tell her. "I'm your mother. I'm Ana Petrić."

Dagmar just stares, her arms limp at her sides. "You're my mother?" I can't judge whether she's disappointed or angry. She hangs back, but doesn't take her eyes off me for a second.

"Well, look who it isn't." Zdenka has sprung out of the living room. I know her at once, because the explosive, argumentative girl I fought with often enough in the past hasn't really changed. Zdenka was never one to hold back. She was always the most determined and aggressive of children. She props herself against the wall and stares me out. "Just what the hell do you think you're playing at?" I would really like to sit down and take a deep breath, but nobody is offering me the time of day. It's all too exhausting and I haven't managed to step over the threshold. Then I notice Zdenka is wearing a pair of my old shoes. I'm convinced of it, although how I can remember such a detail at such a time is beyond me. They are Seventies originals, brown and orange suede, topped with flowers in a matching fabric. Zdenka strides up, chin jutting forwards like a prize fighter about to demolish a weaker contender. "You're not wanted here."

"I've come to see my daughter."

I look over at Dagmar. Her eyes are full of tears, but she's not crying yet. "I want to talk to you, please."

Zdenka delivers a dramatic sigh and turns on her heel. "Your funeral," she hisses under her breath, as she walks past Dagmar.

Rozana remembers her manners and invites me into the kitchen where she busies herself making tea. Dagmar follows me, but stays at a distance, leaning against the fridge. She's still eyeing me as though she were a little hostile creature frightened out of its burrow. I'm struggling over what to say next when someone else walks into the kitchen. The stranger is an Englishman dressed in a smart patterned shirt with cufflinks in the shape of alarm clocks. Dagmar seizes on this interruption to break the ice between us.

"This is Anthony. He's Zdenka's new boyfriend. And he works for the UN."

A flurry of handshakes follows, then, with the exception of Rozana, we all light up cigarettes and indulge in small talk about my journey and its purpose, ostensibly interviewing a President. Anthony has impeccable manners, which help smooth over the raw edges of my unexpected – and unwanted – arrival. He senses the atmosphere and seeks to keep conversation simple and painless, avoiding any hint that I might be on a wild goose chase. He tries to sort plates and glasses for the early evening meal, but Rozana shooshes him away with a tea towel. "Go and talk to Zdenka. We can manage well enough in here without you."

Before leaving, Anthony puts his cigarette out, but mistakes for an ashtray the stoup with Holy water nailed up by the door. Rozana mutters a prayer under her breath. I don't think Anthony is a Catholic, but he realises his grave error in Rozana's eyes. He casts a desperate eye round the kitchen to find something else to distract his hostess and finds it out on the balcony. "Ah, Snow White and her Seven Dwarves. Is that a relic of Zdenka's childhood or yours, Dagmar?"

Anthony smiles at my daughter, but she's not laughing. Rozana drops a teacup. "That, Anthony, is a statue of Our Lady and the Holy Apostles. But there was a strong wind a couple of nights back and St Peter is in the nasturtiums."

A long silence. Anthony blushes, which I've rarely seen a man do before. Zdenka reappears and rescues him. "Mama, stop torturing my boyfriend. He's not up for a sainthood, not until I've finished with him, anyhow." She wraps herself round Anthony and kisses him loudly in front of us all. Rozana is crossing herself and shouting for them both to leave her kitchen. They leave, giggling. Rozana follows with a tray of cups and the teapot. I'm left alone with my daughter at last, but I have no idea what to say or do. Dagmar sits down, lights up another cigarette and asks, "Are you nervous about interviewing the President?"

I'm more nervous talking to her, but I don't dare admit that. "I've talked to him before, when I was a radio presenter. But that was a long time ago."

"When my father was still alive?"

"Yes."

Another pause. It's so quiet, I can hear the ash in Dagmar's cigarette burning.

"But I wanted to see you too. That's why I'm here."

"Why now?"

"I can't explain."

Dagmar turns to look at me. It's not a wary look, but something softer, more generous. I can't meet her gaze. I don't deserve this lovely young woman feeling sorry for me.

"Are you staying around?"

It's a lifeline. She wants to see me again.

"I want to explain, I really do. If you can give me time."

She half smiles. "Don't mind Zdenka. Her bark is worse than her bite. I think she's a bit jealous, if you must know."

"Why's that?"

"She's been like a mother to me over the years. I think she's scared you'll come and shake everything up and it will spoil things between us."

"What do you think?"

"I'm not sure. But I want to know more."

My inquisitive, prying little girl. I remember her hunting through her Uncle's wardrobe before her birthday. She was five years old and so anxious to find her presents, except there weren't any because I'd been sacked from one of my many cleaning jobs. Word had got out about who I really was and that was another opportunity lost. And I needed everything I could get, however awful the conditions. Three, four jobs a week just to earn enough to help pay the bills. But what was the use? Half the time, there was no electricity. And when you were a non-person, no one assumed you needed heat anyway. You were as good as dead and who cared enough to warm up a pile of bones? In the end, Darko had sold his father's fob watch to buy an iced cake and candles.

"Ana, are you all right?"

At this point, I finally break down in tears. Dagmar gently presses my hand and then quietly leaves the kitchen.

Chapter 7
coffee with the Pink Panther
Zagreb, May 1998

Early evening and Zdenka phones, asking me to meet her in the Pink Panther, one of her favourite bars in Opatovina. She's had a breakthrough and discovered something she describes as "crucial" in relation to Elenora Milković. The Pink Panther isn't the sort of café-bar you want to visit unless you're ready to take on its über-cool clientele. Zdenka more than meets that challenge. This evening, she sports a new mini-dress knitted in soft green mohair and high-heeled silver sandals with laces that thread round her narrow ankles and all the way up her calves. She's tied her red curls up on top of her head so that she looks at least a foot taller than usual.

It's a very small café-bar, with hardly room for six people to stand at its counter, but Zdenka has grabbed one of the tables outside, set up on a square of artificial grass carpet close to the door. She's puffing smoke rings whilst working her way through a large folder of papers. I have to tap her on the shoulder before she notices me.

"Fuck, you look like a gnome," she says, squinting down through a fug of cigarette smoke.

I heave myself up onto one of the chairs opposite. Our taste in anything rarely coincides, but I don't hold it against her. The biggest bone of contention is my choice of wardrobe. I like wearing torn net skirts over footless tights with DM boots which I buy from a second-hand store in an alleyway off Gradec. I customize the boots and the skirts with spray paint, strings of beads and tiny religious icons. Zdenka claims I look like I've fallen off a musical box owned by a colour-blind sadist. I say if I was as beautiful as her I would dress in a similar style, but there's no point when you're plain and punky. People would just laugh at me.

Zdenka always retorts that "I need to exert myself more". "Some eyeliner, a different way with your hair. Nicer shoes, definitely."

Tonight, though, Zdenka has her latest discovery to relate. She has tracked down Vesna Skurjeni, an actress who worked with Milković. She has a contact at the National Theatre who is trying to arrange a meeting.

"This could tip the scales," she says, lighting up a new cigarette. Her hair is slipping out of its pins and down her back. One of her sandal's ties has started to unwind and has attracted the interest of a little terrier perched on the lap of the man sat alongside us. He is oblivious to the dog because he's conducting a conversation with a man over the road, sitting at his open window on a first floor balcony. The dog wriggles to be set free and the man releases him. He's straight onto the sandal tie and Zdenka is nearly pulled from her seat. The two men break off their conversation to shout at the dog. A waiter joins in. The dog keeps its teeth fixed on its prize and tries to stare down Zdenka. She's laughing now, because she loves the attention. Just when I think I've got to unclamp the dog's jaws and save the sandal, a stranger beats me to it. The dog's owner orders plum brandies all round and it's only then I recognise Zdenka's knight in shining armour: Marko Strgar. He flashes a smile and toasts me. Zdenka is quick to introduce herself and the conversation soon turns to her latest, favourite topic: her research into Milković's life and times. I'm surprised how reticient Marko is in his replies. Zdenka is ecstatic because she thinks she's made another breakthrough. "Fisković was Meštrović's star pupil. What do you know about their models?"

Marko pauses too long. I don't know him well at all, but I sense he's uncomfortable with Zdenka's line of enquiry. "There were so many," he finally replies. "Where to start?"

"But Elenora was the best actress of her day."

"It's just tits and bums, if you think about it."

Zdenka thumps the table in her exasperation. "That's not how it is! Fuck, it's someone's life I'm talking about here, someone subjected to outrageous misogynistic behaviour, but still making her mark. The kind of prejudice you obviously endorse…"

"Don't be so quick to judge me, please."

Good God, Zdenka has met her match. But she loves arguments. She debates ferociously, her corkscrew curls spinning around her face like tiny fiery demons. Men usually fall in love with her and other women fade into the wallpaper. Interestingly, Marko doesn't conform to the general rule. He sits quietly whilst Zdenka vents her rage against him like a thunderstorm.

"The point is, what is the point?" he asks. "Elenora Milković might have faded into obscurity for a reason that can't be summed up by the words "male conspiracy." She might just have had her day."

Zdenka nearly spits out her drink in disgust. I realise it's time to intervene before blood is shed: "But there's something else you've found out about Elenora, isn't there? That's what we were going to talk about, before you showed up, Marko. Zdenka is going to meet with someone who knew Elenora."

"What?"

Marko's air of composure, unaffected by Zdenka's outburst, is suddenly disturbed. Zdenka notices his change in manner. "I'm meeting with Vesna Skurjeni. Day after tomorrow."

"I see."

"Have you heard of her? Or is she another pointless female in your grand scheme of things?"

"I have met with Vesna several times."

This reply silences Zdenka. The pair stare each other out, like a pair of territorial robins. I think I've worked out the problem: they are treading on each other's patch; both are working on possible groundbreaking discoveries about two very different Croat artists and are keen to keep any honour and glory for themselves. It's like the troglodytes at the university all over again. Zdenka had better watch out. She finishes her drink and turns to me. "Let's take a walk, Dagmar. I need some air." And ignoring Marko, she sweeps off her bar stool and starts to walk down the street. I hover for a while longer, anxious to smooth over the argument. I have my own reasons for not wanting to upset Marko. "I'm sorry about Zdenka," I say, "but she's always had to fight to get what she wants."

"No need to apologise. I like opinionated people, as it happens. You know just where you stand with them."

"No mistaking what Zdenka thinks, ever."

Before parting, I ask if I might meet him at the gallery to talk about the Fisković retrospective. He gives me his number and tells me to ring him later in the week when he's back from Split. "I'm going to see Fisković," he reveals. "I'm hoping we can finally settle on a chronology for the exhibition's layout. But don't hold your breath."

"He's still alive?"

"The old bugger is indeed alive and kicking."

For some reason, I thought he might have died after he stood the President up and turned his back on his own painting, the one that for many symbolizes the greatness of the Croat nation. (Except Zdenka, who thinks the sitter for the portrait was probably paid in stale herrings and ripped off for eternity.) Outside, the evening has advanced and the nightly ritual of corso is far advanced. Families and strangers mingle and parade in the streets, stopping at cafés for drinks and icecreams, or window shopping designer fashions. Zdenka has been waiting for me at the end of the street. When I appear, she suggests we stroll in the direction of the Cathedral. As we walk, I feel that the whole city is on the move around us. Many refugees came here during the war and they have stayed on, some from choice, but many because "choice" has long since become a redundant option. These displaced people must spend their new lives rotating around the city's streets, night after night, like a special breed of human night owl.

We pass by the Cathedral, which is undergoing repairs, like many other buildings in Kaptol. The main entrance is flanked by a number of badly chipped angels who lean in towards each other as though in conversation. The rim of an old clock face has been abandoned alongside them. It looks like a rusty Polo mint. Many of the houses around the Kaptol are still in a terrible state. Rubbish has been stuffed into splintered window frames and doorways to keep the dust and rain out; the iron grilles over the ground-floor windows are also packed with debris. Some still have their original wooden shutters, the kind that open up from the ground. A man in a beret peers out of one of these shuttered windows as we pass and waves his pipe in silent adulation of Zdenka. She skitters along on her spiralling silver heels like a dazed water spider. We stop at another café close to St Mark's and order bottles of Jamnica water.

"Just imagine if I do get to talk to Vesna," Zdenka continues. "What stories she'll have to tell."

"What if she's senile? What if she doesn't want to talk?"

Zdenka dismisses these concerns with a flick of her cigarette. "I have a feeling in my bones that she will and then I'll have the meat for my thesis. Don't spoil it, please. Not just because you've fallen out with the Rock Star."

This is how she refers to Josip. She thinks he's a loser. I'm beginning to wonder if she's right. We've not really made up since that day at the gallery. Zdenka is convinced I should drop him and she'll introduce me to one of Anthony's friends. "But you'll have to borrow something from me to wear, of course."

I don't take up her offer. Nor do I take her advice not to see my mother again. Zdenka has refused point blank to discuss her reappearance, just warning me that she left once before, so she'll inevitably leave again. "And who will pick up the pieces then? Yes, yours truly. Besides, you know she's only turned up because of her bloody interview with the President. She's filling in time, or wasting it, depending on your point of view."

And maybe Zdenka is right? What can my mother really tell me now about either herself or my father, after all this lost time? I feel my eyes water and pretend it's Zdenka's cigarette smoke. Catatonia is playing on the radio in the background and the waiter is glued to an episode of Dynasty showing on the tiny TV screen he managed to wedge in between the espresso machine and the liqueur bottles. I know I'm being self-pitying, but I can't stop myself. Zdenka suddenly raps the café table with her rings.

"Have you been listening to anything I've just said?" she demands.

I shake my head. Zdenka is cross, but she's not unkind. She knows I'm thinking about my parents. "Look, we need to get out of Zagreb," she says, wrapping my hands between her own. "And I've got a plan." When has Zdenka ever not got a plan? I smile through my tears. "Anthony's put some work my way, in Hvar. There's a theatre festival on the island and they need a translator. It's been organised by the British Council. Okay, that's where I come in. I'm going to translate for a director from Wales. Grand, eh? As for you, well, if you want to turn up your nose at a holiday in the sun then that's your funeral."

"What holiday?"

"The director wants a cast of real people, not wanky, over-demanding professional divas. It sounds amazing. And I've put your name forward."

"You've done what?"

This is a horrendous prospect, because I'm terrified of an audience. But Hvar is a place I have long wanted to go. Before the war, the Dalmatian islands were a choice holiday destination. Even Aunty Rozana went there once with her friends from church and she still goes on about its beautiful setting and the open-air concerts staged by a Franciscan monastery. She bought us little silver bracelets decorated with turquoise beads that had been sold on the harbour wall. I'd like to see the place for myself. I'd like to eat grilled octopus at a café under shooting stars and listen to the boats in the harbour as they rattle and sway in the breeze. My daydream is interrupted by Zdenka sneezing.

"There's work going at the island hotels, so you won't be out of pocket," she says, wiping her nose on the napkin that came with the water bottles. "Besides, you need to get away from the Rock Star. Make a fresh start. Who knows what might happen?" Zdenka's eyes gleam at the prospect of an adventure. She's bored too, even with a UN lover to wine and dine her. "And there's something else. Hvar is about an hour and a half from Split. And Split is where Antun Fisković is living, according to your new best friend Strgar. We can maybe pay him a visit. See if he remembers meeting either Goran Petrić or Elenora Milković. One in the eye for Strgar, either way."

She knows she's got me hooked. She even offers to buy me a new dress to celebrate. It's close on eight o'clock and I hope the shops will have closed by the time we finish our coffees, but Zdenka hauls me into a boutique nearby and forces me to try on a tiny crochet dress with bell sleeves that she saw standing to attention in the window earlier in the evening. It fits perfectly, even I can see that, but I'm self conscious before the mirror. It's like I'm looking at a poor pretend me. Zdenka and the boutique owner, however, are ecstatic. The boutique owner is gaunt with iron straight, platinum blonde hair. She wears a microscopic dress made out of what looks to be lime green PVC and huge platform wedges. "You're the spit of Audrey Hepburn, isn't she?"

Lime Green Lady turns to Zdenka for confirmation, not me. Zdenka nods her head vigorously and puffs on her cigarette. Lime Green Lady produces a tiny pair of silver ballet pumps and insists I try them on to. "You must finish an outfit, *zar ne*?" Zdenka continues the conversation on my behalf. I slip the shoes on and I must admit I like them more than I do the dress. They'll work with my ballet skirts and leggings. Lime Green Lady scoops up my abandoned clothes and throws them in a filigree metal bin by the cash register. "Out with the old, in with the new, darling." She then disappears behind the dressing room curtain with Zdenka to consult over some other garments, leaving me alone in my borrowed finery. I twist and turn in the mirror. I seem to have stepped into someone else's life, stranded with the wrong script and the wrong costume. I sit down, rest my chin in my hands and watch in the mirror as tears pour down my cheeks.

Chapter 8
lost & found
Split, November 1934

The winter rains were exacting their toll on everyone's nerves. Days of incessant rain, which leaked in at badly fitting windows and doors. Every room in Fisković's narrow stone house seemed to reek of damp clothes steaming gently on lines strung above the stoves. Antun sought refuge in the workshop, but the cellar had flooded and a large number of stone blocks needed rescuing. He helped Fisković lever them from the cellar, working up to their shins in the stagnant water that swirled in through the cracks in an ancient drainage system. They spent one fruitless morning trying to chase out the rats which clung to the stone blocks like shipwrecked survivors.

Fisković was unperturbed by the delays following on from this disaster, but that was because he delegated most of his unfinished commissions to his son. Antun was holding fast to his decision not to return to college, so he was obliged to finish the trumpet-blowing angels and a host of other celestial beings destined for the grander houses off the Peristyle. Wealthy Splićani commissioned dozens of archangels and saints to decorate their magnificent porticos, so much so that Antun struggled to keep up with demand. The poor, on the other hand, commissioned what they had always commissioned from Fisković & Son: a modest headstone for a modest sum, carefully squirreled away inside the pockets of ancient sheepskins. Antun occasionally took liberties, throwing in the odd decorative flower, or twist of vine leaf, as part of the fee. He felt he owed these proud people some kind of gesture. Fisković gave Antun precious few dinars for all his hours of labour, but he deserved this punishment. No one had forgiven him his refusal to return to college. Even Jakob was avoiding him, but it wasn't easy, because he had asked Antun to help restore a number of carvings in his warehouse. Antun took a secret pleasure in working for Jakob, often chosing to stay late into the night, because he felt in this way he could pay back what he owed in wasted study fees.

He also admired the craftsmanship he found on all four storeys of the slowly disintegrating building which made up Jakob's home and warehouse. The curly haired stone lions on the first floor were a particular wonder. A whole pride seemed to occupy the pediments above each window; he imagined them to be one family, dominated by the male lion that held up a coronet of vine leaves in his wonderfully modelled teeth. The heads were reliefs, which had probably been salvaged from a much earlier site, possibly Roman, or Pre-Roman. Stepping down into the basement, Antun passed sphinxes and unicorns carved in richly coloured marbles and glossy ebony. Jakob collected these sculptures on his many travels abroad and Tilde gave each one a name, convinced they came out to play when all the traders had left and she and her father were tucked up in bed. She shared her made-up stories for each carving with Antun as she passed him tools or a chamois leather.

Jakob had told Antun many stories about Split when he was growing up, how it had once been a city that existed underground, its citizens a population of busy little moles thriving in its Roman ruins. Antun wondered if that's why he liked working in the warehouse's basement so much, because it made him somehow closer to that long-ago time. He liked the gloom of it and the buried treasures; he liked closing in on a piece of stone, focusing on a detail that another had carved centuries earlier. Tilde shone the storm lantern over his kneeling frame, catching her breath as though worried it might spoil the work in hand. He had spent several weeks attempting to restore the body of a phoenix, replacing its damaged wings with a new pair worked up in bathstone. Tilde held her breath for minutes at a time as she watched him work. She was practising, because she wanted to live underwater. Branko had told her that whole cities lay buried off Dalmatia's coast and she was very keen on living in a house of coral and going to work on a seahorse.

"What happens if a fish swims into your bedroom?" Antun asked.

"I'll club it to death and then cook it," she replied. "Branko's shown me how. One very quick blow, you know, so it's not cruel. They don't know a thing, really they don't."

He made her a fish out of a piece of driftwood, which she carried round, balanced on her shoulder. "So he can listen in to everything that's important," she explained.

Antun made more carvings for Tilde. He didn't really think of them as toys, because Tilde was twelve going on ninety. Jakob shook his head. "You were Meštrović's heir and now you make gee-gaws for a child."

Jakob had a point, but Antun couldn't listen to his reasoning anymore. He was in mourning and so was the rest of the courtyard, but for very different reasons. His neighbours were still in angry uproar over the news of the assassination of their King, overseas in Marseilles. Antun's reaction, however, was different – he feared Milan had been involved in the attack. He'd heard nothing from him for months, but what if he'd taken a boat to Marseilles and plotted such a terrible thing? As far as Milan was concerned, the means justified the end. King Aleksandar's hated dictatorship had only proved one thing to him, that any hopes of a free Croatia were being destroyed by a pro-Serbian government. His hero was Pavelić, a man condemned to death by the authorities in Belgrade. Pavelić had gone on the run rather than face trial for demanding the overthrow of King Aleksandar's government. Milan had often chalked Pavelić's words up on the walls in Zagreb's streets and later had set up anti-Serb demonstrations in and around Jelačić Square and the Academy. The city's police had chased him, week after week; the interior of Antun's rented room, which they shared, was probably better known to them than to members of his own family. Anton had spent a small fortune repairing his door, splintered down to firewood by more than one zealous security patrol.

According to Milan, Antun was a political imbecile, but even he knew the stakes had been raised with the King's assassination. This was regicide, treason and sedition all rolled into one. Jakob read out loud the newspaper reports. No stone was being left unturned to find those responsible for gunning down a monarch in cold blood. Rumours abounded of alliances struck between Croatian independents and Bulgarian and Macedonian terrorists. Jakob felt the tide had turned and he was no Canute. "The future belongs to such people, so what is left for us?"

He hugged Tilde to him, but she was indifferent to his fears. She was going to set sail with Branko any day soon. He had promised a day on the waves. The city'll be just like Split," she had decided, "except everything will be decorated in coral beads and fish eyes. We'll drink out of seashells and wash ourselves with sea sponges."

Jakob sent her on her way and sat down with Antun to share a small plate of radishes and cheese. Antun offered up a bottle of white wine he had left to cool in a dark corner.

"What do you think will happen now?" Jakob asked, nibbling on a radish with his very white, very rodent-like teeth.

"I think I will be carving a lot more tombstones."

"You don't think it's important to make a stand in another way? To make something that will challenge – and outlive – such brutalities?"

"Who can say what will survive such things. I don't know that Meštrović has the answers anymore than I do."

"He says you knew Milan Gregorević. Please, Antun, you're not of his persuasion? That isn't why you left Zagreb, is it? You're not in danger?"

Antun sipped his wine slowly, considering how best to answer. "I left because I couldn't see what purpose was served by my staying," he said, at last. "I lost confidence in my work."

"And Gregorević?"

"He shared my room for a while. We knew each other from life drawing classes. He modelled sometimes to earn money for his studies. He was having trouble with his rent, his landlord, any number of things, but no Macedonian agitators, from what I can remember."

"He was an artist?"

"Well, he took some classes with Meštrović, but he wasn't really that committed."

"Maybe a cover for his other activities?"

"Do you think I'm in danger because I helped him out with his rent?"

"No. I think you're in danger because of what people might assume from that. I know you would have acted in good faith, but too many others will see a conspiracy there – even if all you did was share a charcoal stick."

Antun refilled Jakob's glass. "As far as I know, his only crime was to imagine he was the painter Manet's equal."

Jakob laughed and drank his wine, but then became serious again. "If there is trouble brewing, you will tell me, Antun? I will always be your protector. It's a promise I made, many years ago."

Antun was startled by Jakob's intensity. After all this time, he didn't need to keep reiterating his obligations. The encounter troubled him for several days. He avoided going to the warehouse and chose to work instead on individual pieces in Fisković's workshop. It was hard to keep the place heated now that November had come, and the first flakes of snow. Antun worked the larger commissions to keep moving, stretching and bending to accommodate scale and detail. He was working up a laurel wreath on an angel's brow late one morning when there came a low whistle at the half-open door. He was expecting Fisković, but instead a man in a battered trilby hat and a slack old overcoat walked in. Antun could smell his unwashed skin from the top of his stepladder. He assumed the stranger had come about an epitaph for a tombstone. He took his time, easing the stone dust out of an incision he had just made to create the spine of a leaf. The man stamped his feet and blew on his hands. He was muttering something under his breath.

"What's that you're asking?" Antun called down.

The man looked up. His face was gaunt, the skin tinged an ugly shade of grey suggesting hungry days and sleepless nights. It was a minute or two before Antun could believe what he was seeing: it was Milan, back from who knew where, his Renaissance beauty transformed into this vulpine creature. "I'm asking if you're ever going to light a fire in this shit hole? And is there anything to eat?"

Antun, still shocked, smiled. This was the Milan he recognised, one quick to demand his needs were met before offering any explanation. He hurried down the stepladder and set to work building up the fire in the wood stove. He took his coat, which he had left hooked up behind the door, and wrapped it round Milan's shoulders. The other man's fingers were red raw with chilblains and the nails rimmed with dirt.

"Where have you been?" Antun asked.

A mixture of shyness and repulsion kept him from touching the filthy hands, so tantalisingly close to his own. Antun took his satchel from the peg on the door and rifled through it for cheese and bread. Milan barely waited for him to offer the food before he ripped through it like a starved dog. Antun felt tears build but worried at crying in front of Milan. He'd never liked tears, or kisses, or gentle touches. Antun had to force himself to turn round and stop staring at the trembling, shabby figure.

"I need a boat," Milan croaked through a final mouthful of half-chewed bread.

Antun knew he could never ask anything of Milan without more pain and loss. But still, in spite of the awful smell and the wretched look of the man, he couldn't help but want him. He reached out and touched Milan's cheek. The bone felt as hard and as cold as the stone he'd just been cutting. "I'll get you a boat," he said. "Where are you going?"

"It's better you don't ask."

Milan propped himself against the back of the door and closed his eyes. A few seconds later, much to Antun's surprise, he smiled, a shadow of his old, brilliant smile. "No more questions, Antun. Can I catch some sleep here before I go?"

It was decided that he would go already and yet they had barely spoken. Antun hadn't time to reply before Milan slipped down to the floor. He watched him sleeping for several minutes. Antun knelt down, took a deep breath, and then leant in close. The face, so familiar and so damaged all at once. He kissed his eyelids, his bony cheeks, the jutting cheekbones and his lips, but Milan didn't stir.

Chapter 9
the man in the mask
Zagreb, June 1998

The President's Communications Director explains there has been a change of venue for my interview. It's now going to take place at the Mimara Gallery, in front of the famous portrait of a young Croat fisherwoman by the Split-born artist Antun Fisković. Apparently, the President ranks it as one of his favourite paintings. The gallery is hosting a retrospective for the artist early next year and the Communications Director feels it's too good an opportunity to waste. "She's our Joan of Arc, if you think about it."

It's a large claim to make, as unlike Saint Joan, the Croat fishergirl has no history, not even a name. So much has been projected on her thin shoulders, it's a surprise she can still stand upright. In truth, I don't really like the painting currently propped up on a wall in the gallery where we're having our meeting. The girl is too ethereal and delicate to be convincing as a labourer in Dalmatia's pre-war fishing industry. She stands gazing out of the frame, a fishing basket strapped to her back and two dead mackerel hanging from a piece of twine in her left hand. One of the straps is tied round her head, and I can sense how much it digs into her skin. She wears the distinctive red stockings of the islander and a pair of rough clogs. Her hands are red, as if she's finished salting the catch, but to my mind they are the hands of another woman superimposed on her own finer, more delicate-boned wrists.

Goran knew her name. He'd winkled it out of Fisković towards the end of his stay in Split and had rung me late one night to discuss his discovery. The girl was a Jewess. "Just think of that," Goran said. "Fisković painted the spirit of Croatian womanhood – and he used a Jewish model for the job. A real smack in the eye for the fascists."

Even today, the woman's identity might be unpalatable for some in our country. Goran had never published his revelation; in fact, I believe he took it to the grave with him. And I'd forgotten about it, until today.

After my world had turned upside down, a painting of a long dead fishing girl had been the least of my concerns. It amuses me to think about Goran's revelations now, as the enthusiastic Communications Director parades up and down in front of the original painting and exalts its political credentials.

"Croatia comes of age and it's time to celebrate the contribution of one of our greatest artists to the cause. He's still alive, you know. He's lived in comparative obscurity for decades, but the exhibition promises to pay him his due.

I wonder if it would be politic to ask if that "obscurity" was self-imposed. Fisković was a troubled man, I know that from things Goran mentioned in our nightly telephone chats whilst he was away in Split. He was associated with Pavelić's Ustaše, with the Independents, and even briefly with the Communists.

"Artists are often very private people," the Communications Director observes, as she comes to a halt in front of me and hands over a list of the questions I have submitted to ask the President. There are a lot of alterations scrawled in red biro. "Take a look and come back to me if there's anything you don't understand."

The woman is statuesque and elegant, like a cover model but without the cosmetic veneer. She doesn't suggest there will be any negotiation over the President's edits. It's as I expected. I note she doesn't give me a date for the proposed interview. There are still "unexplained complications" with his diary and I'm given to understand that these might yet scupper any arrangements. I'm about to leave the gallery when a man calls out: "Excuse me, but are you here for the exhibition press conference?" The stranger is very insistent when I say no and make my excuses. "It's the first time the portrait has been shown to the world since it was abandoned in an office basement. The conference will tell the story of its miraculous recovery."

"I'm not here about the painting. I'm here to make arrangements for my interview with the President."

The stranger, who hasn't actually introduced himself, comes to a halt beside me.

"You're Ana Petrić?" He looks at me, curious. He's very beautiful, but pretends to play the shy bystander. He apologises for holding me up, his hand nervously tracing his collarbone as he does so. Something about his behaviour intrigues me, in turn. "Marko Strgar," he says, holding out his hand. "I work at the gallery." We shake hands and he escorts me out of the building into the little park. "It's not everyday I get to meet a legend from Croatia's media," Marko says. "You were part of Maspok, like our President. Fascinating times, I'm sure."

"I doubt you were even born then."

He smiles, but dismisses my compliment. "I think it's important that my generation doesn't forget what went before."

It's a safe, comfortable generalisation, but it's not what he really wants to say. I sense Marko has another agenda. Maybe he wants to get into journalism, or to find out information for a thesis? It seems to be what every twenty-something I've met recently is keen to do, even members of my own family. He invites me to dinner and I accept, because it's been a while since anyone offered, let alone a beautiful young man. My second marriage has come to a blisteringly ugly conclusion, largely thanks to a young editorial production assistant my husband employed right under my nose, with a view to "releasing me from administrative hassles". In fact, I'd been released from my marriage, had been put to one side with all the compunction of a weeks' old dirty plate. If I fool myself with this stranger, so what? I've earned a respite from the depression that has followed in the wake of my divorce, like a buzz of angry mosquitos. Marko takes me to a restaurant in Opatovina, one that is trying hard to emulate the boho chic I've seen in some of the Western cities I've visited recently. Huge red chandeliers hang above our heads, whilst our chairs are mock antique, re-upholstered with loud prints featuring horses, skyscrapers and, most incongruously of all, portraits of Audrey Hepburn.

Marko lays out his stall with confidence. We smoke, drink champagne and avoid revealing anything too personal. Tonight, I'm a woman who can still fall for a man, even if I'm well into my forties. Marko plays his part like an actor, holding my gaze, regardless of the other, much younger, and stunningly lovely women floating by; he keeps a gentle touch on my wrist as he reaches for a sauce or an olive. Tonight, I re-invent myself as Ana Petrić, stylist and editor.

This version of Ana has never had to cope with the fall-out of civil war, or a divorce.

My new admirer lives close to Opatovina in his own apartment. I know Marko must have connections very high up with the Government to live in relative splendour like this – his own place, and no unruly relatives cluttering up its rooms. My former brother-in-law and his family are forced to squeeze into a similar sized space. Marko pushes the bedroom door shut, his muscular back pressing against the soft fabric of his shirt. The room is lit by clusters of church candles, set out on stylized metal dishes. I glimpse a big square bed littered with pillows and a crumpled throw. Marko asks me to undress. He lies on the bed and watches me, intent as an eagle. His face in this subdued light is hard; the shadows giving mystery to his eyes and cheekbones. It's as if he's wearing a mask. I stand beside the bed, hesitantly. I can't read his face-mask. He crawls over. His fingers are suddenly inside me; I can feel the pressure build, as I steady myself, leaning into the bed. When he suddenly pulls me down on him, I'm like a slip of fabric, moulding myself around him. He's going through a ritual, but he's generous enough to make it feel more intimate, waiting for me to come, or to change position so I can keep his mask-face before me. I'm drawn in, like a stunned fish on the end of a line and he knows it, but doesn't dismiss me.

"Ana," he whispers. "Ana Petrić." The woman I was, the over-worked Slovene editor and miserable divorcee, is obliterated under his busy tongue and fingers. This is what he is giving me, not just sex; I'm wanted for being nothing else than this: a woman who can lie with a man without any fear, or reluctance, or anger because of the past.

When the candles burn down, Marko's bedroom takes on the appearance of a smoky chapel. The weakened flames are reflected in pools of wax and the expensive abstract pictures on the walls above are just black hollows. Marko's body is a stone weight, leaning in against my curved back. For the first time in a long while, I feel completely at ease. It is a precious gift, but it will be short-lived. I wait for Marko to fall asleep, and then I dress and return to my hotel by taxi. He texts me the next morning and I see we have an understanding. "Goodbye, Ana Petrić. And good luck."

I ring Dagmar's mobile next. I feel back in control and ready to answer her questions without my former defensiveness. I know I've been evasive and it's time to deal with that, particularly in my dealings with my daughter. We have a few minutes of desultory general chat, before I ask if we can meet. Dagmar suggests we have a coffee in the Pink Panther where she's arranged to meet Zdenka later that same afternoon. She keeps me waiting and I begin to doubt her intentions. Can you stand up your mother? By the time she arrives, I've settled my tab and am pulling on my jacket.

"Sorry. I missed the tram."

She orders a coffee and then hands me a photograph. It's a picture of Goran, taken about two months before he left for Split. The shock of seeing it again, in the middle of this pretentious, noisy bar doesn't help my mood.

"Did he want me, Ana?"

I have to ask her to repeat her question over the noise of the speakers positioned close to our table. The stupidity in trying to discuss such a thing in these surroundings overwhelms me. "He didn't want anything," I snap back at her. "What else to tell you? He left this world long before he died."

"Did he know you were pregnant?"

It's a simple question, but I can't immediately reply. Dagmar's gaze cuts into me. I knew she'd ask me this, but I thought there might be time to prepare an answer.

"He didn't know, did he?"

"He couldn't understand things, not at the end. It would have been futile – "

"It might have made all the difference."

Her look shames me and yet infuriates me. She knows nothing of what either Goran or myself went through and I can't begin to sum it up over an espresso and a cigarette. She's looking at old photos and wants to play happy families. I pick up my handbag and slip off my stool.

"You didn't want me, is that it?"

I pity her confusion but I can't find the words I need to complete this conversation without delivering more pain. I try to think of a reassuring exit line, but I'm interrupted by the arrival of Zdenka. She's none too pleased to see me, nor does she pick up on the atmosphere, but immediately launches into an explanation of what she's discovered. She's been to see the actress Vesna Skurjeni, the source she hopes will lead her to Elenora. Vesna is, apparently, sick with cancer and close to dying, but Zdenka would seem to have called at the right time, when she's ready to put her house in order and give up the secrets that have weighed on her conscience. A new Croatia, a new world, so why protect the old any longer? ·

"She gave me a letter," Zdenka says, temporarily abandoning her cigarette. "Elenora wrote it to her son. It talks about a lot of things: the horrific experience of having to give away her only child (she shoots me a meaningful look when she mentions this) and what happened to her career when the Serbs came under attack in the city in the Second World War. But what's most interesting is the memories of her relationship with her child's father." Zdenka sits back on her bar stool and blows out a perfect smoke ring. She checks to see that she has our complete attention before continuing. "Elenora's lover was married. And he was a Jew." She checks her notes. "Yes, he was called Jakob Eschenasi, and he had a warehouse in Split before the war. So, Antun Fisković was the illegitimate love child of a Serbian actress and a Jewish trader. And this at a time when either label could be a death warrant." Zdenka fiddles with her cigarette. "I think my thesis is going to be really something," she adds. "Fisković is the key, if I've read all this right."

Zdenka rattles on about her meeting, but it's just small details that don't really absorb me, not in the way her mention of the merchant Jakob Eschenasi has just done. Memory is a strange commodity, one minute operating like a floodgate open to the waves, at other times, a barricade that nothing can penetrate, even the most vital of questions or answers. And sitting in the Pink Panther, I start to remember something that has been niggling at me since the day before when I'd been shown "A Portrait of Croatian Womanhood". The girl with the wrong feet and hands; the pretend fishing girl with a thick leather strap rubbing her forehead raw. Her name was Tilde. Tilde Eschenasi. I'm able to confirm Zdenka's discovery, but I'm afraid too. The sense of control I had after my night with Strgar has evaporated. Fear is a punishing legacy and it was fear, I know, that kept Goran silent on his return to Split after interviewing Fisković, not the later edict of a discredited Croatian Communist Party trying to deny him his humanity. Goran's discoveries in Fisković's atelier had even worried his colleagues on *Croatian Weekly* and they had tried dissuading him from writing about the artist and the complicated legacy of his birth. Goran's daughter and his niece are playing with fire, but I don't know how best to warn them.

Chapter 10
Saint Prospero
Zagreb, May 1998

After my unsatisfactory meeting with my mother in the Pink Panther, I hope to have better luck with Marko Strgar. His office at Mimara is little more than a cupboard, furnished with a fold-up table and two white plastic Starck chairs. He's made an effort to create a sense of space by avoiding shelving or filing cabinets. A brand new Apple laptop and a pot of coffee are the only objects on the table.

"A minimalist by nature, luckily," he says, ushering me in and pulling out one of the chairs. "I treat it as a think tank, and my office is out there." He waves an arm in the general direction of the gallery. He pours coffee and then flips open his laptop. "I've something to show you." The computer whirrs into action and Marko deftly opens up a series of files. He finds what he's been looking for and swivels the screen in my direction. I see a reproduction of a pen and ink drawing of a nude woman. The drawing has been completed in a few masterly strokes, suggesting the knot of the woman's black hair coming undone and slipping down her spine. She kneels on a stool and looks back over her shoulder. It's a study from a life drawing class, by the look of it.

"It's by Antun Fisović," Marko says. "Circa 1933."

"Something for the exhibition?"

"Possibly. It's a drawing of the artist's mother, Elenora Milković."

"He drew his mother naked?"

"I doubt he knew he was doing that. He would have regarded her as a model earning a few dinar, nothing more. Not at that time anyway."

"Didn't he ever get to know her?"

"Later, but by name only."

I stop to reflect, making another inspection of the drawing as I do so. It's a confident drawing. I've never been very good at drawing from a model. It was something I had hoped to improve on by going to college, the same college Fisković attended, but then the war started and I needed a job. I share that information with Marko. He smiles.

"Fisković was a master in ways people can only guess at. Much of what I'm doing at the moment involves documenting and archiving his paintings. Not the set pieces like that blessed portrait of the fishing wench, but private paintings with much more of a bearing on our brave new world."

"How do you mean?"

"Fisković's real life's work – and this is his own claim – is to record the old tales from Dalmatia. First and foremost, he regards himself as a true-born Splićan, not a Croat. He paints the stories told to him by the fishermen from the islands and the stories he listened to in his father's workshop in Split. Stories told to him in the dialect of the islands, in čakavski. He claims he paints stories because he hardly knows anymore what language to tell them in."

Marko clicks open another picture file, this one showing a detail from a large-scale painting. It's of a white deer standing against a backdrop of highly stylized trees. It's a wintry scene, the trees bare of leaves, but the shadows at their roots are a dance of purple, green and blue. The head and body of the deer are shown in profile, but its one eye looks out squarely at the viewer, as if the animal had been painted from the front. It's a weird effect, enhanced by the fact that the eye is a blank oval. I remember my father mentioned something about snow deer in one of his tapes. Marko explains it's one of Fisković's key works and will form a centrepiece for the new retrospective. "It's based on one of the old island stories. I forget the details."

Marko strikes me as being the most meticulous of researchers, so this claim sounds false. I've got more questions for him, so decide not to challenge this. Instead, I start telling him what I have learnt from my father's tapes and from my recent conversation with Ana. He listens attentively, but doesn't comment until I finish speaking. "And what else has Ana told you?"

"Nothing really. She's not happy with me digging around in my father's past. There were all kinds of accusations around Fisković and they damaged the Maspok cause. Well, that's what she says."

"Wrongful accusations probably, but mud sticks." Marko clicks again and shows me a series of costume drawings. "Fisković turned costume designer just the once, for a performance of *The Tempest*. Dalmatia's Italian occupiers thought the locals might want to celebrate their ignominious status by putting on a play by Shakespeare. A play about a nation state coming into being, what could be more appropriate for those experiencing their first taste of independent rule? Except it was a rule overseen by Germany and Italy who carved up the bloody country like a butcher's carcass."

"Did the play get put on in Split?"

"No, in Hvar. There's an extraordinary theatre there, do you know it? Well, it was the first public theatre to be built in Croatia. Back in 1612. And, by coincidence, a Saint Prospero's bones are also buried on the island. Here's Fisković's representation of Shakespeare's magician Prospero, and this one shows Ferdinand who ends up marrying Prospero's daughter."

I note the leather jacket, the necktie, and the patched moleskin trousers. To my mind, it looks like one of the pictures of Tito's victorious Partisans which used to adorn our school history books. Marko seems to read my mind. "My hunch is it's a portrait of Branko Ostojić," he continues. "He was a Partisan hero and a fisherman from Hvar who knew Fisković from boyhood. This particular drawing must have been a very deliberate provocation to the authorities and Fisković knew it. He was defiant in the only way he knew how, through his art. The designs caused uproar by all accounts. I think once people understand the risks he took they will understand he was never an Ustaša."

"Were these designs ever used?"

"Yes, but they had to be altered on the strict orders of the Italian commander in Split. It didn't stop them. The island women making the costumes sewed hammer and sickles into Prospero's robes and the jackets of the ship's crew."

"My father mentions a cloak on his tape."

Marko leans in closer, and it feels as if the room has grown smaller too. I'm conscious of his leg pressed against mine, our hands nearly touching by the laptop; the smell of tobacco on his breath and something else too, a citrus scent, maybe an aftershave. His hand brushes mine, but I don't know if it's by accident. He's used to persuading people to do what he wants, it comes across in his confident air and relaxed gestures. "Would you lend me the tapes, Dagmar? You can see how valuable they might be for the exhibition. There might be material we could use in the catalogue. We would, of course, acknowledge your father's contribution."

He doesn't doubt for a minute that I will hand over the tapes, but I do resist him, which surprises us both. I'm not adept at arguing or being confrontational, like Zdenka, but I can be quietly stubborn. I don't really understand everything I've listened to on my father's tapes, but I do know I want to come to that understanding for myself. It's part of my discovery of my father, and *not* Fisković. He's a means to an end. I try and explain this, but Marko is impatient and butts in. "How many tapes are there? It might take a while to transcribe them."

"I'm not sure. Quite a few are damaged. The bedroom was damp where they were kept."

Lying seems the only way to stop Marko hassling me. I shift my hands out of reach and pick up my rucksack. "I'll see what I can find back at the apartment and let you know, okay?" Marko slips back into his previous charming self the minute he senses victory. He steers me out of the little office, the palm of his hand resting gently against the small of my back. "I'd be very grateful for anything you can lend me. Give me a ring, anytime."

Back at the apartment, Zdenka erupts halfway through my account of my meeting with Marko Strgar. She's against the idea on principle. "The principle being, he's a womanising bastard. And Anthony's had a look at Strgar's background and he's got a whole lot more to say about him." Zdenka swivels round on her high-heeled silver sandals and gently kicks Anthony's shin by way of a prompt. He shifts forward in his armchair and fills me in. Strgar is the son of one of Tudman's cronies and it's a case of like father, like son for he has worked those connections to the uppermost.

"He left to study at the Sorbonne when Croatia voted for independence. He saw which way the wind was blowing, and that war was inevitable, I suppose. A contact at the office says he's very close to the President, in spite of that. I don't know about this exhibition at all. It feels like it's part of some kind of propaganda campaign by the government and it might be best to steer clear."

"Or rescue the truth," Zdenka interrupts. "That's what Dagmar and I want, not more lies and subterfuge. And we're getting close, that's why Strgar is rattled."

Anthony rolls his eyes. Preaching caution with Zdenka is like trying to negotiate with a runaway bull. I'm not sure about Zdenka's stand, but I do know I feel closer to my father as long as I'm following in his footsteps. Zdenka has another battle on her hands altogether, similar to the one she took on with the university authorities that banned her plays from being staged in the early 1990s. She was often forced to put them on in our apartment instead. Their content hadn't helped – polemical outpourings about the iniquities of what was happening on the political stage. When sanctions loomed after Croat artillery blew up Mostar's historic bridge, she'd written a satirical diatribe challenging Tudman's leadership. It had been banned before she'd even written the last page. I remember sitting on a cushion in the living room watching her then boyfriend play Tudman. In one scene, he'd hoovered the rug. Aunty Rozana sat beside me, fretting. "Why's he doing that?" she'd whispered. "People will think I didn't clean up beforehand."

"It's symbolic, " I'd replied. "He's supposed to be representing the President sweeping bad news under the carpet."

Zdenka disappears to find alcohol to calm herself down, leaving me with Anthony. I perch on the arm of his chair and he wraps one of his long arms round my shoulders. He's wearing his clock cufflinks again. I can hear them tick, tick ticking away when I lean in close. Anthony is kind and he never lectures (unlike Zdenka) and he looks so handsome in his cobalt blue shirt. I hope Zdenka doesn't break his heart, or worse, argue him under the table. Anthony, I know, is someone I can confide in. "When I found my father in Uncle Darko's suitcase, it was as if I could really get to know him at last." Anthony nods. "And that's what I want. I'm not really interested in conspiracy theories, or whatever else Zdenka thinks is happening here."

"I understand," he replies. "There are so many different kinds of grieving, inflicted in so many different horrific ways. Christ, it's shit out there, it really is. Sometimes, I just want to run away from it all. But I'm lucky in another way. I'm still alive and I can prove that conclusion wrong to some degree."

Which he does, over and over again with his work in the UN controlled zones. Zdenka sees him as some kind of Shakespearian hero, standing centre stage and restoring order to the world with a shake of his briefcase. Anthony knows it's a more nuanced role; he doesn't grandstand, and he rarely discusses politics with anything like Zdenka's certitude. I know he finds it difficult to reconcile his love for Zdenka with acceptance of her one overriding fault: an unconquerable need for drama in her life. Zdenka can't understand how others don't share her perspective. What Anthony is doing is nudging her towards that understanding by his own example; it's what Goran was doing too in his interviews with Fisković. Probing and reassuring him in turn to find out the truth.

I turn back to the tapes later that evening. The tapes are the pathway through all this, that I do know. *I paint the detail of the everyday*, Fisković explains in a tape dated October 8, 1971, labelled in my father's neat, italic handwriting. *The tragedy of the man who loses his life at sea, the women running to the harbour to see if it's their loved one dead on the shore. The island women's hands are scarred from their gutting knives. Have you seen them? Wonderful, expressive hands....* It sounds as if he's telling a real story here, and I know I can only fully understand it by going to Dalmatia to find out for myself. On this point at least Zdenka and I are in full agreement.

Chapter 11
grandfather Fiskovic's saddle
Split, November 1935

Antun had returned to his father's atelier, for in truth, he'd not had any clear idea what else to do once Milan had fled into exile. He assumed his former lover was still in Italy and still causing trouble, but there had been no word other than from Branko who confirmed he'd set him down on shore at Ancona, as requested. This chapter in his life closed, Antun realised he had little choice but to finish his course at Zagreb and return home to assist his father. The Fiskovics hadn't been young when they adopted him, and now their age was telling against them. He'd delayed his departure home to complete two new pieces for a mixed exhibition before packing up his things to be sent on ahead by rail.

His only mistake was to arrange to return on All Souls Day, along with the whole of the rest of the world, or so it appeared. Antun planned his first port of call to be the little whitewashed cemetery in Split where the Fiskovic's ancestors had been buried for centuries. The latest addition to the family crypt was Antun's maternal grandfather. The latter stages of Antun's journey were made partly by cart and partly on foot, because he had run out of money halfway to the coast. Moving to Zagreb, Antun had always regretted giving up riding. His grandfather had taught him, late one summer, walking him round on a lunge rein until he was confident enough to take his hands away from the saddle's pommel and ride headlong into the wind. Long, hot afternoons spent tracing circles in the dust.

Grandfather Fiskovic had always kept a horse, a couple of goats, a cockerel and hens. Without them, his family would have starved during the wars that had welcomed in a new century. He had built his home by hand out of the derelict foundations of an old shepherd's hut, not far from Senjska. There had been no electricity, and water had come from a roadside well. Even though he had endured all these hardships, his grandfather, to the best of Antun's knowledge, had never experienced the ignominy of wearing out his shoe leather trudging along badly kept mountain roads. Antun had lost the sole off one of his boots, following a particularly long and winding hairpin bend downhill.

He stopped and removed his boot. His feet were sore and hot, even though the air around him was cold, with the threat of snow. He replaced the boot and wound his scarf round his sole to keep the whole thing intact for a while longer. In half-an-hour or so, he would be in Split itself. He decided to cut down towards the Marjan Hill and to Senjska direct. He'd made good time, in spite of the boot's collapse. Close to Senjska cemetery, there was a small square where the men of the district gathered for an evening drinking plum brandy. That night, the square was far busier than usual. Antun had immediately been accosted by Mile, one of his grandfather's old drinking partners, sat snug on a bench outside a bar, glass in hand.

"Antun? It's been a long time," he said, baring his few remaining teeth.

They shook hands and exchanged news. Mile had, as usual, bought a bunch of roses and a new candleholder for his dead wife. He did the same thing every year, unlike Antun's mother who this year had combed the city to find the right orange flowers, the right piece of greenery, even a funeral sash which she wanted to drape over grandfather Fisković's headstone. Antun's progress through the square had been slow, because there were many other people who recognised him and stopped to chat. Everyone was keen to hear about his exhibition. It had been written up in the newspapers and much had been made of his participation. Antun felt awkward as he listened to everyone's congratulations.

Reaching the cemetery, his mood of introspection worsened. He felt as though he was walking backwards in time and coming to meet his boyhood self. Each row in the crypts in front of him was swarming with families brandishing ladders, cleaning rags, votive vases and armfuls of flowers. By nightfall, thousands of candles would be lit, illuminating the hundreds of headstones, many of them barely legible under the tidal wave of floral tributes, china icons and faded photographs. Antun lit a cigarette. There was no sign of his parents, so he decided to make his way to their house in Narodni Trg. By the North Gateway, two old women in headscarves were selling walnuts from open sacks. He bought some of the nuts, served up in a cone of newspaper, and crunched his way through them as he made his way down the narrow street leading to his home. The edges of the stone houses touched his shoulders. Some had their shutters flung open to let out the steam from stews boiling on fires. He could see an old woman looking down on him, a small clay pipe wedged between her gums. He winked at her as he passed by and she clapped her hands in delight.

At the end of the street, he turned right into Narodni Trg. The Fiskvovićs had lived under the Clock Tower for hundreds of years, probably ever since its first bell had chimed. As a boy, Antun had fallen asleep to the sound of bells calling his neighbours to evening Mass, then woke to hear them ringing again, summoning latecomers to morning Mass. He was always late, infuriating his mother even though he almost slept under the hands of the Clock. Antun arrived at the family's apartment block and looked up to see a light shining through the lop-sided wooden shutters. He hunted in his pocket for keys. Like many of the other buildings in the street, the entrance door had seen better days attached to a more splendid mansion. It was made out of a thick piece of timber, and bound with huge iron hinges shaped like some kind of supernatural plant. As Antun fiddled with the contents of his overfull pockets, his father burst out of the door, still issuing threats to someone over his shoulder. His parents were arguing – again. "Thank God you are here," Fisković announced, slapping him on the back. "You can keep your mother sweet for me."

He knew his father was heading to the bar he had just left, probably to drink away the night with Mile and his compatriots. Antun embraced his father and headed up the stairs to the apartment. The entrance to the hall was partly hidden behind a fly curtain made out of clacking blue beads. He had to push it aside in order to find the lock. Inside, it was almost pitch dark, except for the dim red light given off by the votive candles in the parlour just ahead. "Mama?"

She appeared from the direction of the parlour, a few stray petals from some unseen bouquet decorating her plain black outfit. She burst into tears when she saw him, but recovered herself almost as quickly.

Antun noticed her creased hands, the skin as thin and delicate as the petals she was plucking from her sleeve. Her legs were bent and she seemed to have trouble walking. She dismissed his concerns. "It's your father who needs running after. And where are you then?"

After a small supper of cheese and olives, and a change of boots, Antun escorted his mother to the cemetery. They joined the hundreds of people gathered there, the scene alive with colour and candlelight. The air seemed less wintry, because of the heat of the candles, and by the glasses of plum brandy that were circulating between families and friends. Antun stood by his grandfather's headstone and found himself recalling old stories he thought he had long buried. He remembered the saddle his grandfather had bought for his first grandson, complete with silver-chased triangular stirrups. He had saved for years to buy the saddle – long before a grandson had even been born. When Antun had arrived rather unexpectedly in the Fisković home, he had inherited the saddle. Guilt cut through him, like a whip's stroke. He had sold it last year to pay for Milan's passage to safety.

The brandies kept coming round. Antun leant against the crypt for support. He saw the shapes of people moving in front of him, round and round, like busy flames dancing on fire. Suddenly, a hand reached out from the dizzy whirl and shook him hard. "Antun!" It was Branko with an invitation to join him. He had sought him out specially, having come over from Hvar earlier in the day to sell his mackerel catch. Ignoring his mother's look of disappointment, Antun left with his friend. They staggered down to the square below the cemetery, singing and laughing and sharing a couple of cigarettes they rolled as best they could in a doorway to avoid the wind that had blown up. Antun was drunk, but not so drunk he couldn't suggest a plan of action. He wanted to find his grandfather's old house, once a fair distance from the city, but now swallowed up in its ever-expanding streets. He would know it when he saw it, he assured Branko.

They set off along an unlit road leading away from the square. The sky was littered with stars, so they had been able to keep their footing. They even watched a falling star appear briefly above them before fizzling out behind a roof decorated with Roman statues, dressed in togas. Grandfather Fisković's house had been built on the stretch of coast leading away from the Marjan Hill. Below the house, a series of terraces cut into the rugged stone of the coastline. On one of these terraces, Antun had learnt to ride. The lower terraces had been left a wasteland after his grandfather's attempts to grow olives and almonds had failed. Once, they had visited the very bottom terrace, jutting out above the crashing waves. His grandfather had tied him to his chest with a thick rope and lowered them down. Antun could remember it even now: the terror and excitement of plunging feet down into a world beyond the one he had always known, a torch strapped to his head to light his way. At the bottom, they had found a little stream and a handful of stones stuccoed with the bones of ammonites.

"Perfect," his grandfather had said. "Only stone and water for as far as the eye can see."

All these years on, Antun and Branko settled by the edge of the same rocky descent, close to the remains of the old house, where they proceeded to smoke and talk.

"Can I tell you something?" Branko said in an unusually subdued voice.

Antun wondered if this might be some kind of turning point for them both. This close to Branko, he imagined the smell of sea salt coming off his skin. But what his friend said next completely threw him. "Gregorević is dead." The world tipped. Antun had to put his hands down to steady himself and to stop himself from falling over the edge. "I was in Ancona, this week just past, on business. My father has made contacts at the harbour there, opening up a new market for us," Branko ploughed on. "I heard something when I was there, told to me by a man I trust completely. Gregorević had many enemies, you know, and not just here in Croatia."

"Please, tell me everything."

Long minutes passed. Antun took several deep breaths to try and stop his body from shaking. Branko remained silent so long his friend wondered if he might have fallen asleep. "There was a brawl and Gregorević got a real kicking. He died in the street where he fell. People didn't like his politics, or − "

"Or what?"

"There were rumours. That he was too fond of his own kind, if you see what I mean." Branko rolled over onto his side and rested a hand on Antun's leg. "I'm sorry, but there it is. I thought you should know, because you need to be careful. You were his friend and there are some who might assume you shared his views." He paused before continuing. "He was an Ustaša when all is said and done. And there are many, like me, who oppose what such bastards believe, because we think the Serbs should be our allies, not our enemies."

Antun felt the heat of Branko's palm against his leg, like a brand. He wanted to jump up and run away; he wanted to absorb the shock of his news alone. No, what he wanted was to avoid having to think about his friend's guarded warning. Had he guessed what was really afoot? The fact that he touched him without any awkwardness probably meant not. Branko was all concern, his disgust reserved for the fact that a man could be murdered in a street brawl and then left to die like a rat in a gutter.

"Where did they bury him?"

"I've no idea. That's all my friend could tell me. But what I say is this: forget him, Antun. Forget him and stay home where you belong."

Chapter 12
conversations with Our Lady
Zagreb, May 1998

It was Ana's idea to meet at the open-air shrine in Gradec dedicated to Our Lady. Our last encounter had been so disappointing, I was glad when she rang and asked for a second chance. Approaching the stone gateway which houses the shrine, I notice the pews are full and several more people are standing in front of the statue of the Virgin. Nuns move silently amongst those praying, each carrying a tin pail filled with bundles of fresh candles. Each of the thick yellow candles is decorated with pictures of a garlanded Madonna. The candles are lit throughout the day and left to burn down into a metal basin, creating a permanent bed of molten wax that glows bright, challenging the glare of natural daylight beyond.

It's no ordinary shrine, and that's why I know my mother chose it. Since the war, it has become a place of commemoration. Mourners come and pray for their dead out in the open for everyone to see. No hiding history here. Reaching the back row of the pews, I spot a man on his knees, clutching a photograph against his chest. Tears pour down his cheeks, but no one intervenes. Grief is expected. The figures sitting in the pews are in shadow and I can't make out Ana's features amongst them. People pray quietly, but their pain is no different from that of the kneeling man. A nun stands in the doorway of the shop close by, selling religious memorabilia: tiny lamps and candles, some thick as logs, some bearing the red and white check emblem of a new Croatia. There is a poster of the national football squad propped up against the display of little lamps. My father didn't die in the war, but I still sometimes sit on one of the pews and pray to his memory. I don't know if he was a believer in the way that Aunty Rozana is, but I want to think of him as existing somewhere, even if not here on Zagreb's streets. It's a feeling that has intensified since I heard him speak on the tapes. I hover behind the pews and wait for a space to become vacant. This time, it's my mother who is running late.

The man kneeling in front of the shrine bends forwards until his forehead touches the ground. The nun with the pail glides up and places her hand on his back. She whispers something, but the man doesn't move. She pats his back and joins the nun in the gift shop. Then a hand touches my shoulder and I jump back, startled. Ana has arrived and is silently beckoning me to join her at a table outside the café over the road. It still feels odd seeing her after such a long absence. Ana has changed into someone else altogether whilst she's been away, and she's no longer just my mother and Goran Petrić's widow. No, it's no good. I can't call her "Mother".

It's not just her appearance that stops me, although that has markedly altered. Photographs Aunty Rozana has shown me reveal Ana Petrić once dressed like a Seventies model, all floaty frocks and lace-up Victorian boots and a top hat with a band of lace and flowers. Today, Ana is wearing something a lot more expensive and tailored, probably by Jil Sander, or Armani. She's always raving about their collections in *Neu Style*. She has filled out but her broad shoulders and long legs mean she gets away with it. Her shoes today are fantastic creations, bright green satin with red cherry fastenings on the ankle straps. "She always turned heads," Aunty Rozana told me once. "I was so jealous. But she paid a high price." I grew up thinking of Ana Petrić as some kind of ethereal sprite, tormenting and confronting the dreary-suited men in the Croat Communist Party with her decadent Western fashions and brilliant argumentative nature. Goran was a maverick too, banned from his first job in journalism because he turned up in green velvet loon pants and white plastic platform boots.

"That's when he and his friends decided to set up an alternative," Ana says, spearing a piece of grilled squid on her fork. "*The Croatian Weekly* was linked with the *masovni pokret*. Did you ever get taught about that at school?" I shake my head. I learnt tidbits from my Aunt and Uncle, but most of all I learnt to keep quiet about who my parents were, or what had happened to them. "The Croatian Spring, the Maspok movement," my mother continues, "was all so simple. We took to the streets to demand recognition of the Croatian language. That's how it started, Dagmar, with a row over a Serbo-Croat dictionary, which we all felt favoured the Serbian language above our own. But what it represented was something much bigger, the belief that the Communist Party in Croatia should have more representation in Belgrade's government; that we should redefine Yugoslavia's constitution and try and stop our taxes being spent elsewhere and our friends being forced to go overseas to find work."

Ana abandons her squid when she starts recollecting the heady days of summer 1971, when she fell in love with my father and political revolution at one and the same time. "We believed in change from within the Communist party," she continues, thumping her wine glass down. "We were not saboteurs, like they claimed. Tito, the Old Man, ruled the roost and maybe there was a time for that once. But we believed Croatia should have her chance to walk on the world stage. And that art could play its part. That's what Goran was really interested in, the way in which artists like Antun Fisković could portray a generation's dreams and ambitions. But our enemies were stronger than us. They claimed we were in contact with Ustaše exiles and were planning to bring about a second Fascist state." I want to hear more about the street fighting and my father's journalism, but my mother has gone quiet. *The past is a dangerous place.* That's what Marko Strgar had said and his comment is reflected in the tears that slip down my mother's cheeks. She's lost in some complicated memory I can't possibly share. But I do understand the significance of being labelled an "Ustaša."

"We wanted truths that would restore our sense of identity; maybe win more power at the top table and assert our own laws. Was that so very terrible, Dagmar?"

Ana is openly crying now, and the diners sitting around us are getting embarrassed. Maybe they've heard what they shouldn't have? I sit, self-consciously, wishing I knew what to say to comfort Ana. I wonder if mentioning the Fisković exhibition at Mimara might distract her. Ana refills her glass whilst I rummage through my rucksack to find my notebook. The postcard of Fisković's "A Portrait of Croatian Womanhood" is tucked into the back pocket. I hand it over to Ana and explain how the tapes have inspired me to find out more. For example, what my father was hoping to discover when he travelled to Split to meet with the legendary artist. Ana's hands shake when she picks up the postcard.

"I had no idea your uncle kept any of Goran's tapes. That was a huge risk to take."

"Do you want to borrow them?"

Ana glares back at me. "Listen, Dagmar. I really wish you would forget this idea of finishing what your father started. You'll be much better off going to Hvar and meeting a rich Italian or German, or finding a future for yourself. I doubt there is much of one here."

She hands back the postcard refusing to discuss the subject further, reverting instead to small talk about my travel plans. I can't bear the pretence any longer. I get my purse out of my rucksack, ready to pay my share of the bill and leave, but Ana unexpectedly stays my hand.

"You think I'm being unfair? Well, let me tell you one more thing and, hopefully, you'll see why this is a dead end. Goran's investigative journalism became a liability. Mostly because of his interest in Fisković and the artist's links with some of the Ustaše's most despised supporters. Men like Milan Gregorević, who planted bombs and thought nothing of the people he might maim or kill. Years later, it gave the secret police a lot of ammunition when they turned their attentions to closing down *Croatian Weekly* and condemning its writers as Ustaše sympathisers. Your father included. Many people were wrongly implicated and they paid a terrible price."

"Maybe this is a chance to put things straight?"

Ana shakes her head. "Goran found out things, some of which could still cause ructions, even today. It's not worth re-opening it all again, believe me. The past isn't something that sits quietly on display in a museum. It has the potential to destroy, right here, right now."

"Well, I'm meeting with the curator for Fisković's exhibition later and he might well tell me what I need to know."

A silence follows. Ana is weighing up whether I'm calling her bluff. She finishes her wine and wipes her mouth with the edge of a napkin. "It's playing with fire, the whole thing. Please, let it rest and live in the present. You're lucky to be able to do that, if you could only see it."

I file the postcard away in my notebook and wait for Ana to say something else. She seems anxious to speak, but she's unsure of herself. I think about what she's told me and realise it might be the very same thing that Marko Strgar is after, the truth about Fisković's birth, the twists and turns of history – and the mixed legacy of his sculptures and paintings. And then something else occurs to me. Elenora Milković gave up her only child, just like Ana did. Frustrated by her reticence with me, I try and push her further. "Did Goran ever find out why Elenora gave her baby away?"

"Think of the times," Ana says, after a short pause, her hands gripping the top of her handbag tightly. "She might well have been a native of Zagreb, but she was booed off the stage because she was a Serb. She had no work and war was about to break out. She was regarded as the enemy within, like Goran and I were once upon a time." I sense Ana's vulnerability and reach out and put my hands on top of hers. She doesn't look at me, but stares down at our joined hands. "And it was the same for me. I wish I could make you understand, but I won't be able to. It was another lifetime. And you are who you are, Dagmar, and I've got no right to interfere. Maybe it's just as well I'm going back to Slovenia at the end of the week."

"You're my mother. That doesn't change, even if everything else has."

"It's too late," Ana says, her voice hardly more than an angry whisper. "I know it, even if you don't. The idea that I can just waltz back into your life and all will carry on as if nothing ever happened. I'm more likely to see the prayers over at that bloody shrine being answered by a cavalcade of angels."

I suddenly realise that the man I saw kneeling at the shrine has stopped by our table. He's still holding his photograph and he is still crying, a grown man, maybe in his late fifties, or early sixties. He leans over, tears dripping off his chin. "Where will I find the future?" he begs us, his voice broken with despair. "Where can I find it, please?"

Chapter 12
the moth and the fisherman
Split, 1935 – 1938

Antun returned to Split as Branko had urged him, and soon after, his father's health deteriorated dramatically. Fisković was now housebound in the family's apartment near the Clock Tower and Antun found himself running the workshop in addition to realising his private commissions.

His first solo commission had come from Split Council. He was asked to carve a statue of Vinko Pribojević, a sixteenth-century Dominican friar from Hvar. Pribojević was one of the first people to lecture about the history of the Slavs and the validity of the Croatian language. But what should have been a triumphant recognition of Antun's homecoming quickly disintegrated into open argument. Opinion was split between those who believed the commission represented a stand for Croatia's call for Independence and those who thought it revealed the artist's bias towards the exiled Ustaše Croatian Revolutionary Organisation. The so-called *dotepenci* living in exile in Italy heralded Fisković as a true Patriot – and a man after Pavelić's own heart. What got lost in all the arguments were Antun's actual influences when he started drawing up his designs. Nor had it helped that whichever way the mould of his statue was cast, Pribojević always ended up with a big head.

"He was an intellectual, so maybe that's why," Branko suggested. "He's speaking to you from the grave: give me authority, Antun; give me bigger ears."

It was rare for Antun to meet with Branko in the months following his return. Branko travelled to Split less frequently, more often than not leaving his sisters to sell his catch at the harbourside. His journeys now took him in the opposite direction, to Ancona where he met with new friends he'd made in the harbour's bars, friends loyal to the Communist cause. "The comrades tell me our Prime Minister Stojadinović is playing Italy off against Germany and losing to them both," he'd told Antun one night. "He's offering them our islands, like a tasty dish of frogs' legs."

Branko kept notebooks in the pockets of his old sheepskin, recording the debates he took part in which sometimes reflected on Antun's alleged links with the Ustaše. When they did occasionally meet for a drink in Split, it was usually after Branko had been to a clandestine meeting with local patriots who shared his desire for the islands' independence. He would open up his notebook and mark out particular lines for Antun to read with a bruised thumbnail.

"I learn the important things off by heart," he explained, "But comrade Mario writes them down for me, so I can share them with people like you who can read. This is what Mussolini claims, that the islanders are Italian, because they speak Italian. No mention that we were forced to hold our Croat tongues in order to survive. Thousands went into exile during Venetian occupation rather than starve. Our fish and our oil were replaced with goods sent in by Venice's chosen traders. But still we were taxed to the limit – and for what? So they could pay bribes to the Turks on the mainland and keep them at bay. This is the history of my island, Antun. Hvar was the bastion that kept the Turk from invading the West. The blood was emptied from our veins, and the gold from our purses. And history repeats, that's what Mario tells me." Branko flourished the notebook in Antun's face. "This is my country, even if it is ransacked by upstarts. I will defend it, just as my ancestors did."

The sea change in his friend's thinking frightened Antun. Branko's diatribes reminded him more and more of Milan's angry rhetoric, and look how he had ended up, murdered in a gutter outside a bar before he'd even turned thirty. Despised and condemned, not even a headstone to his name and he a stonemason's son.

"Will there be a war?" he asked Branko, shocked at the prospect.

His friend shrugged. "Mussolini refuses to hand Pavelić over to our Government. And so the *dotepenci* mock us, because they are getting off scot free even though they murdered our King Aleksandar. And our Prime Minister does what? Pops over to see Hitler and gets pissed at a banquet, like a school boy who can't stomach his first drink."

One night, Branko had called Antun to a bar off the harbour at Split where he was meeting with the comrades. He wanted Antun to talk through his latest designs for the Pribojević statue – more particularly how it could celebrate the islanders' history. Antun had finally decided to cast Pribojević in his friar's robes, holding open a large antique book to commemorate the writer's championing of scholarship and learning. Antun barely finished his statement when uproar broke out around him. Branko had lumbered to his feet, twisting his bolero to fit more comfortably round his broad shoulders. "The truth of the matter is, we know what Pribojević's book should say and that is: to hell with all occupiers. Every man shall stand free."

Toasts were drunk in quick succession to Marx, Pribojević, Branko, Antun and to all who sailed on the sea and had at least two decent nets to their name. Lidija, the whore, was also toasted as she wandered into their corner of the bar. Branko seized and embraced her, to the cheers of his friends. Antun was close enough to hear the sticky suction of their kisses and was disgusted. Lidija lurched out of his drunken embrace and fell backwards across the table in Antun's direction. He saw, with horror, her breasts slipping out of her dress and threw his jacket over her face and shoulders. There was more uproar. Lidija threw the jacket away, squealing like a piglet, and it was all Antun could do to stop himself from blocking her mouth with his bare hands. She reached over and caught his face between her fat fingers. "I've not fucked an artist before, so what about it, Antun? I won't charge nothing."

Antun felt sick. He grabbed his jacket and hat and ran out of the bar ithout any particular direction in mind. Someone was running to keep up with him. He shot up a narrow alleyway and out into the Peristyle, nearly falling over a net of peaches left out on the flagstones. A hand reached out. It was Branko. He'd run after him in his shirt sleeves and was still holding a bottle of plum brandy.

"Antun, please wait. Look, I'm sorry, things got out of hand back there, but it was just a joke. You mustn't take on so. We're just rough, simple folk compared to you Zagreb artists and – "

"Stop mocking me! I was born and bred here. I don't deserve to be treated differently, to be sneered at."

"I expect the girls in Zagreb are a lot prettier and daintier than our

Lidija." Branko thought he'd discovered the root of the problem and slugged back the dregs in his bottle by way of congratulation. Antun leant up against the nearest wall and lit a cigarette. "You must have had some rare fun up there." Branko slumped down on his heels and looked up at his friend. "There are girls like that, aren't there, soft and gentle as summer moths? I dream of them, Antun. Women with the eyes of a Madonna, but everything else in full working order!"

Antun gave a half-hearted shrug. He had no idea how to talk to another man in this way, even after years of trying.

"I've seen one, just like that, here in this very street. Can you believe it? A tiny moth girl. Eyes like almonds and a mischievous smile. But I daren't speak to her."

"It's not like you to hold back, my friend."

Branko's face softened. Antun wondered if this was the look he himself had worn when he raced up the stairs, three at a time, to the room he had once shared with Milan, hoping to find the other man stretched out on the truckle bed, naked and ready –

"I'm in love with Tilde Eschanasi," Branko cut into his daydream.

It took a few seconds before Antun realised what Branko had just confessed. He was in love with the daughter of Jakob, his patron. But surely she was no more than fourteen or fifteen at the most? He tried picturing the mischievous sprite he had known his whole life, transformed into the kind of woman Branko had just described.

"Tilde is clever, Antun, just like you," Branko continued. "She reads books about everything, not just silly stories. She will always be out of my reach."

"Maybe in a few years' time, you will be able to speak to Jakob."

"Antun, Tilde is a Jew. It's not that *I* mind, not at all. I can pray in my church, she can pray in her synagogue. It should be that easy, but it never is, is it?"

The months passed, and Antun had been sidetracked with the technical problems thrown up by the casting of his statue in a local foundry. The next time he'd met with Tilde, it was at the reception held in the cellars under the Peristyle, marking the unveiling of his statue. It had been nearly a year since Branko had made his confession, and Antun had not seen much of Tilde during that time. When she walked up to him to shake his hand, he saw for himself how much she had changed. She no longer walked around in borrowed paste jewels, but was a more subdued young lady, slender and elegant in a neat felt hat and lilac leather gloves. Jakob's appearance gave Antun more cause for concern; it was as if he had transformed overnight into an old man, bent over like a question mark, his robes muddy and wet from the streets. It was unlike Jakob to neglect his appearance.

A few weeks later, Antun offered to go and buy fish from the harbour for his mother. Some people, disturbed at the worsening political crisis surrounding Stojadinović and his Government, were making plans to go into exile. Those without influence sold what they could, lining up their personal possessions along the shoreline in an improvised street market. It looked to Antun as though the detritus of a hundred people's lives had been washed ashore. There were scraps of cheap jewellery laid out on handkerchiefs, framed by mottled old mirrors and broken-backed chairs. One woman had even stretched a piece of string between two palm trees to hang up a jumble of old-fashioned coats and chemises, trousers and shirts. A man in a wheelchair sat by a wind-up gramophone, crying. He was selling his collection of old 78s – including recordings of operas he had once sung himself. He tried a few bars to encourage buyers, but most were too upset by his tears to contemplate a purchase. Antun hadn't wanted to linger, but he couldn't help himself. He stopped to inspect a fan of sewing needles and, looking up, saw Tilde standing beside the tablecloth where they formed a shiny centrepiece. She went red when she saw him.

"Tilde? What are you doing here?"

She fiddled with the belt of her dark green coat which matched her eyes. "Pappa wants us to leave," she said, her voice shaky. "He wants to go and live somewhere where the fascists won't come."

Antun reached out and took her in his arms. The thought of losing Jakob and his daughter was too much. Once she'd recovered from her tears, Tilde explained how her father's business had fallen off dramatically over the past year, leaving Jakob almost bankrupt. The Government was favouring textile traders from Germany. Jakob's contacts in Italy had also dropped off, as Mussolini's influence became stronger.

"But I can help you, Tilde."

She shook her head, some of her old girlish defiance still visible in the set of her mouth. "Pappa is too proud to accept charity. You should know that."

Antun wanted to make more enquiries about Jakob, but they were interrupted by a customer calling out for assistance. Tilde turned round and went red all over again. Antun followed her gaze and saw Branko kneeling down beside the tablecloth, piling up needles into his bare palms. "I'll buy these, Tilde. And the cloth. No, I'll buy everything." Tears poured down his cheeks and the needles dropped all over his knees. "I'll buy everything, if you'll only stay."

Chapter 14
Ariel in combats
Zagreb/Hvar, July 1998

Zdenka has packed enough suitcases and bags to keep her going for at least a year abroad, whilst I've stuffed all my clothes and make-up into Josip's army kit bag. We hire a cab to the bus station and nearly end up leaving two of the bags behind. "You've got the right idea, ladies," our driver says. "Go to the coast and find yourself a millionaire each."

It's a throwaway remark, but hurtful for Zdenka all the same. Anthony has been sent to Mitrovica in Kosovo. There are fears that this is the next country in the region to implode into war. The television news is full of speculation about a liberation army fighting with Kosovan Serbs living close to the Serbian border. We take the bus to Zagreb Airport and I try and distract Zdenka by pointing out some of the quirks of our fellow travellers but she just shrugs and stares out of the window. I admit defeat and return to my library copy of *The Tempest*. We fly to Split and take another bus into the city centre. Our journey takes us through a countryside mapped with small houses wrapped in vines. Pillowcases and duvets dry on the balconies below roofs decorated with sausage-shaped red tiles. Close to the city, huge cranes shadow the mountain backdrop and there's an unsightly sprawl of high-rise flats and cement works. It's over 32 degrees, so hardly surprising to find the area around the bus stop full of palm trees. Zdenka reapplies a very bright red lipstick as the bus comes to a halt, then pulls on a pair of Dolce & Gabbana wraparound shades. In ten seconds flat, she's turned herself into a Fellini beauty. The bus driver signals his approval by personally carrying all her bags and cases to a little café on the harbourside where we wait for the next katamaran to take us over to Hvar.

I'm staying at Hotel Lučić, built during Yugoslavia's tourist boom in the 1970s, a prominent building on the harbourside. My home for the next couple of months is a ground-floor bedroom shared with two others who are also working in the hotel in return for board and lodging. Zdenka is staying just up the road in the same hotel as the show director Eos Parry-Jones and the rest of the artistic team. She leaves me at the reception desk. Hanibal Ugrešić is the deputy manager on duty that afternoon, a very tall, thin man with a deep tan that makes his brown eyes look darker still. He shows me round with all the enthusiasm of a person trying to talk up their choice of coffin. "You've got a balcony, but the screen door is broken. Water is intermittent. There are shortages."

"Is the screen door going to be fixed soon?"

Hanibal gives me a long, hard stare, before replying. "The request has been filed."

The heat in the room is unbearable, even with the broken screen door. I step out on to the tiny balcony and my temper improves with just one look at the view. A large banana tree partly screens a small tree-lined cove in front of the hotel. Waves lap at the shore, the cathedral bell tolls out the half-hour and the occasional ferry klaxon sounds it arrival. Back inside, Hanibal is already on his way out. He warns me to come down early to the restaurant for my first shift, as I need to have my induction before starting work. "It's Friday night, which means Flambée evening."

He closes the door behind him and I throw myself down on my single truckle bed. The other two beds are weighed down with a variety of scattered possessions. I have a discreet nose amongst the things on the bed within reach. There's a heap of vest tops with weird slogans and underneath, a pair of white cut-off jeans, which look like they've been soaked in mud. I go and inspect the bathroom. Toothpaste lines the thin shelf under the square piece of glass propped up for use as a mirror. The shower curtains are mouldy. Various coloured hairs lurk in the cracks of the enamel bathtub and in the plughole. I make a note to wash in the sea. There is no air conditioning, no breeze, nothing but a scorching dry heat which leaves me breathless. I lie down on my bed again, and the next minute I know, I'm being shaken violently awake. Opening my eyes, I find a complete stranger looming over me: she has sharp features like a polecat's and badly dyed hair in varying shades of brown and red.

She's only wearing her underwear: a string thong and push-up bra decorated with rose buds.

"You're supposed to be at the induction," the stranger says loudly in my ear. "You can't not do the induction." She strips off her bra and starts rubbing deodorant under her armpits. "I'm Dubravka. And I've got someone coming to see me in a minute, so you've got to go."

I quickly run a comb through my hair and check my make-up. Dubravka has pulled on one of the vests from the bed and a pair of tiny denim shorts. She's busy applying a false eyelash when there's a knock on the door. A young man with a mop of wild black curls walks in. She giggles and drops the eyelash into an open pot of Nivea cream. "Fuck, you don't want to see me like this," she says to the man. He ignores me, as if I were just another side lamp, and leaps onto Dubravka's bed. She's on to him the very next second. I make my exit fast. Down in the restaurant, Hanibal is sitting mournfully by the huge plate glass window overlooking the harbour, surrounded by dozens of German tourists. They have travelled to Hotel Lucic in large packs, each with their own itinerary – and each timed to the last minute. "And you, Dagmar, have let them down," Hanibal sighs. "We're behind on the starters."

"I can catch up, really I can."

At this moment, two men strike up the chords of Neil Sedaka's "Oh Carol" from their small performance podium, positioned under a red velvet drape opposite the entrance door. The diners all burst into applause. A couple even jump up and take a photograph. Both the musicians are dressed in linen shirts and surfer shorts. One plays a small electric piano, the other the drums: both ratchet up the volume. I make my way to the kitchen behind the restaurant. The doors are wedged open with crates of very raddled looking vegetables, but there's no air coming in. One of the chefs starts shouting when he sees me and I realise that I need to serve the plates of grilled sardines and salad that are piling up along the counter nearest the door. Off I go, in and out of the swing doors, like a deranged mosquito.

By the time we get to the evening's highlight, I'm exhausted. My hair feels like wet spaghetti and my palms are so greasy I nearly lose a few plates along the way. The restaurant lights are dimmed and a hushed awe descends on the diners as Chef brings out a huge dish filled with what looks to be a pyre of burning fruit. It's the Flambée. The band switches tempo and plays a more subdued version of their opening song, as the pyre is hoisted to head level and walked around the restaurant. Chef is about to complete his victory circuit when he's unexpectedly interrupted by the arrival of Zdenka, closely followed by a woman dressed in a squid ink black dress. If looks could kill, my cousin could quite easily be the next Friday Flambée victim, but she's completely oblivious to the scene she's caused, as is her companion. This must be Eos Parry-Jones, the director of *The Tempest*, which is being staged as part of a festival promoting Hvar's gilt box of a theatre. Eos sports a bleached blonde crew cut and a necklace that looks as if it's been strung together from discarded mussel shells. She strides up to me, the shells and her generous breasts dancing their own tangled rhythm. She wears no make-up, bar a dash of poppy red lipstick. "I've found my Miranda!" she says, grabbing both my hands and squeezing them together so hard my eyes water. "*So perfect and so peerless.*"

Zdenka just nods and makes some notes in a book. Eos steers me to the one free table in the restaurant, ignoring Hanibal's remonstrations about my being needed urgently in the kitchen. "I'm casting," Eos reproves him. "Coffee can wait."

Once we're sat down, Eos starts to describe her plans here. She's caused uproar already by opting to perform her version of the play on the beach, and not inside the theatre. The cast includes a handful of drama students from Zagreb, an employee of Croatian Airways and a group of refugees who have been trapped on the island since the war ended. "I'm introducing a new character, Prospera," Eos explains. "She's Miranda's mother. This is a story about a girl coming of age, a rites of passage adventure. And it's about a new state coming into being, so apt at this point in Croatia's history."

I had no idea a director was allowed to rewrite Shakespeare, but this is performance theatre. I struggle with the idea of getting involved in such a kooky production. Whilst Eos runs through some casting notes with Zdenka, I notice Hanibal eyeballing me across the restaurant, pointing at his watch and the kitchen door in quick succession. It's half-an-hour before my shift officially finishes, so I make my excuses and return to the kitchen. Hanibal grabs my arm as I walk past. "I'm watching you," he hisses. "Don't think you can disappear every evening with Shakespeare's sister over there."

The next day, Zdenka leaves a note for me at reception, detailing directions to the rehearsal room. Rehearsals are timed well into the evening, not only to avoid the day's lazy, hot heat and crowds of tourists, but also to help fit round our various work commitments – the drummer from last night's Flambée evening is also the show's lighting designer and a part-time fisherman. Although it's close to eleven by the time I leave the hotel, it's as if the day hasn't ended because it's still so hot. The stone walls of the Franciscan monastery are pearly white against a dark ultramarine sky, and stars cluster overhead, like a big fat bulb of celestial light. I follow Zdenka's directions and find myself on a restaurant terrace, close to the Arsenal. The restaurants are full to bursting. Before the war, visitors had to pre-book their tables months in advance, so maybe things are getting back to normal, after all?

A group of children opposite me are crouched down, engrossed by something at their feet. I discover it's a wire mesh panel that opens up into a room below the terrace. Inside, Eos and her company are in rehearsal, oblivious to the noise of the dozens of diners eating al fresco a cherry stone's throw from their heads. A young woman is singing. She has a breathtaking voice, which has drawn the attention of the children by the window. She looks all bone and long eyelashes; her skin, the same pale gold you find on the most expensive chocolate wrappings. The stranger sings her words as if they were enchantments. *"Those are the pearls that were his eyes."*

Stepping down into the basement, I discover the singer is called Milica, one of three singer-actresses taking on the role of Ariel. Dressed in a torn lace blouse and combat trousers, she's unquestionably the one closest to Shakespeare's ethereal sprite. Zdenka explains she's one of the refugees involved on the project. Her attendance is sporadic, and her behaviour erratic but Eos is making allowances. "She spent a long time in hiding, before coming here, you see." I imagine Milica tucked away like a lost glass bead, wedged in dark cracks in broken walls. But Zdenka says it was worse than that; Milica lived in a hole in the ground for weeks on end, a hole like a grave, which she dug with her bare hands. Eos signals to my cousin from the other side of the rehearsal room and it's time to turn to the business in hand. We are asked to write down words that best convey our sense of what an island may be. "A real island, or an imaginary one. There are no restrictions," Zdenka instructs, before attaching large-scale sheets of drawing paper to the walls with gaffer tape.

One of the drama students draws a cartoon sketch of a narrow strip of land with a palm tree on top. Milica watches from a distance. When he adds a shark's fin travelling towards the island, she goes over and starts sketching herself. She draws a banner above the palm tree and inside it writes: "I hate the island."

"Do you mean Hvar?" I ask.

She nods.

"I suppose it's far too crowded to count as a real island."

"No, I hate it, because it's not my home."

Her reply reminds me that she is not, of course, a typical island guest. I try and think of something else to talk about, and settle on her unusual necklace. She wears a real house key on a chain around her neck. She explains it's the key to her family home in Vukovar. "When I go back, I'll be able to get in," she says, as if she's just wandered off on a picnic and got sidetracked by a thunderstorm.

But Vukovar was Croatia's Stalingrad. When the city fell in November 1991, it felt as though the war had been lost. Zdenka and I had painted slogans on banners, which we paraded in Jelačić Square, calling on the citizens of Vukovar to stand tall against their so-called "liberators," a mix of Yugoslav troops and Serb volunteers. The Croat Defence Forces in the city had done precious little to restore order to its decimated streets. President Tudman had closed down their headquarters in Hotel Esplanade, but the damage was already done. Milica's house key makes me feel numb. She watches me carefully. "Don't you want to say you're sorry? That's what people usually say."

"I'm not, though. I mean, I don't really know what I want to say."

Her guarded smile seems to tear her delicate golden skin. "Maybe you'd like to visit where I live now?"

"You live on the island?"

"No. I told you, I don't like islands. I live in Split."

We tentatively arrange to fix a visit at the next rehearsal. Milica doesn't always come, because she's reliant on one of the people she lives with bringing her over on his boat. "But it would be nice if you could come, as I haven't really had a visitor yet."

Next morning, I'm thinking about Milica's odd combination of frailty and strength when Zdenka bursts in to the foyer. Some calamity has occurred. For a minute, I assume it's news about Anthony. "No, Dagmar. A body's been found, close by."

We leave the hotel together, Zdenka filling me in as best she can. The body has been recovered on an islet about twenty metres from the hotel's restaurant terrace. The islet is deserted, except for the jagged walls of a collapsed stone cottage. At the harbour, a police boat has pulled up and there are various officials standing around, talking urgently into mobiles. I spot the Mayor in his habitual outfit of shorts and baseball cap. Next to him stands Igor, the fisherman-turned lighting designer. I have an awful premonition and want someone to prove me wrong. I head over to Igor. "What's happened? Has someone drowned?"

"Nothing definite, except they think it's a young woman's body," Igor replies. "They found her close to the smugglers' cottage."

A boat sets off for the islet, carrying various officials, including the Mayor. I turn on my heel and nearly fall into the water, but Zdenka drags me clear. As I nurse my knee, bruised in the fall, I spot a small group standing a couple of metres away. There's a policeman in front of them, scanning the horizon with a pair of binoculars. A very old woman, dressed in widow's black and old fashioned hoop earrings is standing with two middle-aged men, maybe her sons, or grandsons. They are as still as the stones under their feet, as if holding their collective breath until the boat returns. Maybe it's an islander who has died, and not a refugee or a tourist? The old woman starts swaying gently, her arms crossed over her chest, her hands resting on her shoulders. The men reach out and place their hands on top of hers, as if to steady her. She sways faster and faster and then releases the most terrible cry into the morning air, collapsing to the ground.

Chapter 15
eating with bears
Split, 1939 – 1940

New Year arrived and snow lay heavy on the Marjan Hill and on the rooftops around the Peristyle. Old Fisković had passed away on New Year's Day and Antun had inherited his father's workshop. He continued with his private commissions – some of which took him overseas – as best he could, but the world beyond the snow-capped, terracotta tiles of home was proving a treacherous place to trade in, even for a sculptor with the backing of a master like Ivan Meštrović. Antun was becoming more and more unsettled at what he read in the newspapers, particularly the incessant debate about the need to redraw the boundaries of his country. Croatia's ruling body, the Sabor, had been restored, but this wasn't enough for those demanding true independence from the Kingdom of Yugoslavia.

"It might all come out in the wash," said Lidija, on one of her visits to the workshop, bearing a pot of coffee and a freshly baked loaf.

Antun had started using the prostitute from Zagrebračka as a model and she was proving extremely adept, striking the pose of an angel one minute, a Madonna the next. Her endless litany of complaints was less satisfactory. She moaned about the weather and she moaned about the mice that lived in the skirting boards and were constantly hopping to and fro, as if making neighbourly visits. Lidija traded a blow job for a set of mouse traps from a man in Zagrebračka and arranged them in the studio. No mouse was ever decapitated by the traps, however, because Antun sabotaged them when she wasn't looking. Lidija was concerned when she saw they were still empty. "They're the best you can get. Fuck, even the mice are out-smarting us these days."

Lidija teased Antun relentlessly when the day's work was done. Her main line of attack was her claim that she knew who his lover was. Antun tried ignoring her taunts, but Lidija wasn't giving up. One afternoon, resting from her pose as the Magdalena, she announced she'd read the signs from the word go. "She's like a little bird, a pretty little bird, isn't she? It's a shame what she's been reduced to, and her father too. A gentleman from his poor bare head to the worn soles of his winter boots. Good Lord, but there it is; the lovely Tilde Eschenasi has snapped up your heart, just like these bloody traps should the mice!" She indicated the offenders with a wiggle of her foot and they shot away into a pile of firewood. Antun was dumbfounded. "Jakob is a family friend, Lidija. You know that."

"Ah, but friends can be more than just friends, Antun. Don't try and fool a wise old owl like me."

Lidija chewed carefully on another apricot. Her front teeth were loose and rotten and she was scared of them going all together. "Trade will slip, if I look like some old crone," she confided. She shook her cloud of bleached hair sadly, but perked up. "They say Branko Ostojić has turned politician. Imagine, that child of a man heading for the Sabor! Why, I'm more likely to end up there. I could be Minister of Economics. I know what real trading is, don't I?"

She slapped one enormous thigh and laughed her loud, raspy laugh. Antun was struggling to keep up with her disjointed chitchat. "So, Branko has left the island?"

"Well, what I've heard is this: he's left his boat with his brothers and rolled up his nets and headed for Timbuctoo, or somewhere just as daft. The boy's a fool. He'd earn more respect if he stayed catching fish."

Ever since buying Tilde's pathetic little bundle of sewing needles, Branko had been behaving out of character, avoiding his old haunts and friends and choosing to spend his days inland. Some alleged he hunted boar and deer, others, that he ran wild with bears and lived on tree bark stews, but none of this made sense to Antun. Branko was a man of the sea, his bones were surely made of sea salt? Could it be that his secret love for young Tilde Eschenasi was tormenting him? Antun had tried his best to help her since their meeting at the harbour sale. He'd arranged for her to nurse his father in his last months, whilst he took Jakob on as his business manager. The older man's detailed knowledge of import and export regulations had proved invaluable when Antun's sculptures began to be exhibited across Europe. But his old mentor was unsettled by what he was hearing and seeing around him. He hinted more than once that he planned to leave Dalmatia with his daughter. But Jakob's only other blood ties were in Ancona, and Ancona was in Mussolini's Italy.

Another thought occurred to Antun, as he tidied up the atelier for the day. Lidija's assumptions about his love life, however well meant, had the potential to cause harm. Had Branko heard such tales and is that why he'd turned deer hunter? The truth was, Antun was anxious to keep the Eschenasis in Split, because he wanted more than anything to help Branko win his moth bride. A sharp knock on the door brought Antun back to his present. He had just lit the oil lamps for the evening and they guttered badly in the strong draught that welcomed in his visitor. It was Jakob, dressed incongruously in an old suit that had been repaired many times, and a striped velvet coat. Antun brought him to the stove and brewed up fresh coffee. Jakob seemed distracted, almost dazed in his bearing, and it was some time before he revealed the reason behind his unscheduled visit. "I want you to buy the warehouse," he announced. "It's time for Tilde and I to leave. We are a burden on our friends; we have no more reason to be here than on the moon."

Antun tried arguing with Jakob, but he batted his words away like irritating flies. "It's not about charity any longer," he continued. "There is another reason why I turn to you." Jakob paused and several seconds dragged by, punctuated by the tick on his pocket watch. "You are my son, Antun, and it's a son's duty to help his father."

Antun felt as if he were floating high above the workshop, like an angel passing overhead, catching only fragments of a conversation in a foreign language. Jakob took his time to unwrap a small parcel he had brought with him. It was a bundle of letters. "You do, of course, need proof of such a claim and here it is."

Antun noticed Jakob wasn't looking at him, but at the letters, which he stroked gently, absent-mindedly, but failed to pass over. He began his story, quietly but without hesitation. He spoke of an illicit relationship with a young woman whom he had loved but could never recognise as his wife, because he had already been married when they met. There was more: she was a Serb and he was a Jew. "You might judge me harshly for what I then advised, but quite simply we had no other option. Although your mother was prepared – eventually – to give you up, she insisted I find someone we could trust to raise you. Fisković was my choice." Jakob paused. "I haven't told Tilde any of this, because I'm afraid she will despise me for it. I don't take pride in any hurt I gave to her mother Hepzibah, but I am proud of you. And I loved Elenora."

"My mother?"

"Yes. She was the most remarkable person. Giving her up was a terrible thing. More terrible still, giving you up too. And all the time, neither of us able to speak of what we knew, or what we felt. If the world does this to you, you can never love it again."

Jakob's eyes filled with tears. He bowed his head and the letters dropped from his hands. Antun caught them and made a careful study of the sloping handwriting spelling out the recipient's address. Jakob wiped his tears away on the sleeve of his coat. "You must read each and every one of these," he advised. "Discover Elenora for yourself."

"Is she still alive?"

"I don't know, Antun. I lost contact with her shortly after Tilde was born. You might be able to find her, if you wish. She lived in Zagreb and might still be there. She was Elenora Milković, the actress."

Antun blushed when he heard her name. He had known an Elenora Milković, but she had been working as an artist's model at the time. He remembered her clearly; she had been scorned by Milan Gregorević for no better reason than she was a Serb and the lover of Dabac, a government minister in Belgrade. He had several times been forced by Milan to insult the poor woman when they met at corso, or in a café-bar frequented by Meštrović's circle. There had been times when she had tried to speak with him but he'd turned his back. Dear God, he had turned his back on his own mother.

Jakob watched him from under heavy, scimitar-like brows. "You need time to understand all this, make it right in your own way. I will come back in a few days to discuss our other business." He got up and pulled his coat around him, making ready to return to the streets outside. Antun looked up, as his father's hand came to rest on his shoulder. "Remember, this must be kept between ourselves.

I don't think Tilde is strong enough to bear another blow so soon after her mother's death."

Antun nodded and Jakob left the way he had come, admitting another draught which ruffled the edges of the letters. Antun moved close to the lamp and pulled the top letter free. Slowly, he began reading his mother's love letters to his father. There were half-a-dozen, all written at another time of political upheaval, just after the outbreak of the First World War. He didn't know Elenora, of course, but he recognised her loneliness and grief because it was his own. He wept and kissed the letters when they became too much to bear. Pressed to his cheeks, he noticed that they smelt faintly of lavender. The trace of that scent stayed on his fingers and he could smell it again when he woke late the next morning, still curled up in his coat on the workshop floor.

Jakob's revelation was closely followed by Branko's return. He'd turned up at the workshop, his weatherbeaten skin creased with dirt and his clothes wretched and stinking. Branko had run away, because every stone and pediment in Split reminded him of the impossibility of his loving Tilde Eschenasi. He'd worked as a shepherd for a while, but he'd not liked the mountains. He had a hut and a hunting knife and that was about it. He drank too much and got into fights. He'd had to stitch his own wounds. His diet consisted of berries and leaves. There were bears prowling near the desolate shepherd's hut, but they left him alone. "I think they felt sorry for me," he said. "Whenever they found food, they always left something behind as a present." He'd lived in his hut for nearly five months before falling ill and was chanced on by a traveller who had helped him to the nearest town. His appendix had threatened to burst and he'd been operated on in the kitchen of a bar, just plum brandy for a sedative.

Antun brought a basin of water for Branko to wash in. He'd stripped off his ragged shirt and trousers, letting Antun see fresh scarring on his shoulders and a half-healed wound on his lower abdomen. He couldn't help staring at his friend's changed contours. He was leaner, more spare around the chest, but still muscular. He was reminded of the first time he had seen Gregorević in the life model class, the overwhelming sensation of being so close to another man who gave no thought to his nakedness, and the fight against the sudden desire to tweak the whorls of coarse blonde hair curling down to his penis. Branko had washed himself down, standing in the middle of his workshop. Once he was dry, Antun gave him some of his spare work clothes. Branko sat down on a block of stone. "Are the Eschenasis still in Split?"

Branko had caught up with world affairs in the mountain town where he'd recuperated in a room above a tobacconist's. He knew that some Croat politicians were openly negotiating with Italy in a bid to win out over the Yugoslav government in Belgrade; that Belgrade was being threatened with the possibility of an independent Croatia being set up in confederation with Rome. But what if the Ustaše were to take a role in creating such a confederation? "I've heard Pavelić has met with Mussolini. The Ustaše are no longer outlaws. This is serious, isn't it? If war breaks out in Europe, Croatia might well become a battlefield, especially if Italy decides to go all out and annex Dalmatia, regardless. And what hope then for people like Jakob and Tilde."

"Jakob is talking about going into exile," Antun replied. "I'm going to buy the warehouse and transfer Fisković's old business there. Jakob hopes to pay his passage over to Ancona with the sale."

Branko shook his head. "I doubt Mussolini will put out the bunting, will he?"

"No. But Jakob has a brother there and he hopes they can join forces. Maybe they will be lucky and find somewhere on the map they can stick a pin and label it "home".

"And Tilde?"

"She will follow her father, of course."

Branko was keen to see her before heading home to Hvar, and Antun arranged they have supper at the warehouse the following evening. Tilde met them at the door, wearing an extraordinary dress she'd found folded up in a tiny box, buried away inside a linen chest. It reminded Antun of the costumes worn by Greek statues, glimpsed in photographs in the antique volumes in the library back at the Academy of Fine Arts. The dress seemed to ripple across her limbs like a river, changing shape to match each breath and tiny movement. It was a rich blue, a colour that would have impressed Raphael himself. Antun sketched her dancing round the dining room. He was so engrossed he hadn't notice Jakob join them. When he finally looked up, he saw his father was silently crying.

"The last time I saw this dress, your mother was wearing it," Jakob whispered under his breath. "Dear God, first history mocks us, then she destroys us."

Chapter 16
Goran's birthday story
Zagreb, July 1998

When the interview with the President is postponed yet again, I know the rumours must be true. The treatment for his stomach cancer has failed. The warning comes when I approach the President's Communications Director and she avoids giving any alternative dates on the pretext that "her boss must be free to engage with the growing crisis in Kosovo." Even she can't inject the necessary degree of sincerity into her voice needed to pass off such a lie. The insurgents have grouped under the banner of the Kosovo Liberation Army and the country is turning lawless as the KLA battles with the Serbian police. There are threats of NATO air strikes on Belgrade. But this isn't being dealt with by the President, as Zdenka's boyfriend Anthony explains when we meet at the Pink Panther by chance on my return to Zagreb. The President won't do my interview because the ravages of his illness would be all too visible. "Not even the best make-up artist in the world can help him now," Anthony says.

I tell Zdenka's boyfriend I've come back to Zagreb because I've been asked to by the Petrićs. They took their lead from Dagmar who has stayed in contact with me, even though she is now in Hvar, along with Zdenka, rehearsing a production of *The Tempest*. Anthony fills me in on their progress. There is no mention of either of them having met with Antun Fisković. Maybe he's closed his doors to them, or they've been unable to make the trip over to Split? Our drinks finished, Anthony escorts me to Darko's apartment block. My former brother-in-law was never one for confrontation beyond a certain point and I doubt he's changed over the years. He's still a clerk at a local cement factory and a very good one, meticulous and efficient. His papers are in order, he's never rocked the boat, or challenged the authorities, unlike his younger brother. And yet, he's one of the bravest men I know. When our lives fell apart, it was Darko who opened his home to us. Neighbours shunned him, because he wouldn't turn his brother, an officially decreed "non-person" out on the street, or later, his pregnant, grieving widow. He also kept Goran's notebooks and interview tapes, even though they were incriminating because of the ever-changing fortunes of the artist Antun Fisković. Darko's compassion makes him a hero to my way of thinking, but he's not the kind of man who will make the history books. Not like our sick and dying President. He looks awkward when I rail against the iniquity of such judgements.

"Blood is blood," is all he will say, fiddling with the remote control in his tiny living room, as if pushing the right button will project him straight out of my sightline. "What else could I have done? Goran was my baby brother. Always in a mess, even as a child. He was so clumsy he broke everything and our parents despaired because it wasn't easy to replace things. You know how it was."

I do indeed. Darko sips at his coffee and finally fixes his gaze on me. "Ah, Ana. I still don't understand what happened. Such a terrible thing. Rozana prays and that gives her some peace of mind, but me, I don't pray. I haven't prayed since…"

He can't complete his sentence. Darko found Goran hanging in the bedroom he shares with Rozana, just down the corridor from where we are sitting. He was the one who cradled his limp body, and I was so envious of him having those last few, precious minutes with my husband. By the time I returned from work, Goran's body was already in the morgue and the neighbours gathered on the stairways, dark disapproving crows. I walked through their assembled ranks, terrified, holding on to Darko to prevent me falling straight into Hell. Today, I salute Darko quietly with my coffee cup. Rozana has joined us, her face tense. How this tired woman ever got the strength together to give birth to the force of nature that is Zdenka Petrić is anyone's guess. She's nervous because she knows I'm here about money. Darko will have told her what I outlined in my letter.

"Any news of the girls?" Darko enquires, turning to watch his wife as she plumps cushions and smoothes down the antimacassars. The furniture is that which they ordered the month before they married in the late Sixties. It's retro heaven. The cushion's feather pads are thin, even after a robust shaking. I should have bought new ones instead of the espresso machine and cup and saucer set. But Darko loves coffee and I remember how much he suffered in the past from being forced to drink the awful sachet coffee served up in his work canteen. But I have other plans. Darko and Rozana saw their savings wiped out earlier this year when there was a run on Dubrovačka Banka. Several other well-known banks have since collapsed, causing ruin for many. I want to help them, because they once helped me in my hour of need.

"Zdenka says a body has been found near their hotel," Rozana says.

Darko clutches the arms of his chair. His face is also taut with anxiety. "What's happened?"

"She didn't say much, only that it's the body of a girl. Maybe a tourist, or a refugee."

The three of us sit in silence, wondering if this is some poor victim of recent events, driven to do what Goran did all those years ago. Darko shakes his head. "Are the girls all right?"

"They've started rehearsing on the beach."

"On the beach?" Darko shakes his head again. His daughter's antics have always baffled and delighted him. "But surely it's too busy?"

"They work after midnight when everyone else is at the disco. Apparently, one's been built inside the Napoleonic fort. Imagine that."

"Well, well. As long as they're safe."

Rozana wears her rosary wrapped round her wrist and unloops it now to start saying a small prayer, whilst I set out my case to her husband. It's simple, I want to restore their savings with some of my own. "Look, we can call it payback for what I took from you when I came to live here after Maspok." They are not convinced. I have another plan up my sleeve: I will give them the money to pass on to Dagmar and Zdenka to fund their studies. My daughter wants to take up her place at art college which was postponed when war broke out; Zdenka has her thesis on Elenora Milković to complete. Darko and Rozana look at each other after I've finished explaining the terms of my offer. "Zdenka has been like Dagmar's protector all these years. It's largely thanks to her that my daughter has turned into the woman she is today."

They can't argue with that, although I expect Zdenka will try when she gets wind of it. Rozana says it's Darko's decision and disappears into the kitchen. He sits back in the armchair, staring up at the ceiling. "It's very good of you, Ana," he replies. "And we will accept, because as you said in your letter, the past can't keep tripping us up in the present. Someone, somewhere, has to make the decision to act without being caught up in the same old tangle of disappointment." It's the nearest he's ever come to making a political statement in my presence. He holds out his hand and we shake on our deal across the ancient goatskin rug. It's a truce, at any rate.

On my return to Hotel Callas, I stop off for a coffee in a café near Mimara Gallery. Fishing for some kuna notes for a tip, I come across a slip of paper in my purse that I've not looked at in a long while. Goran gave it to me on his return from Split, before the world turned against us. He was broke (as usual) and hadn't been able to buy me a birthday present. Instead, he'd asked Antun Fisković to write down a story for me, a story that was inspiring him to paint what he called "his true masterpiece". It was a very old story from Dalmatia, one that had been passed on to the artist by the stonemason who had adopted him as a baby. I remember Goran reading it out loud to me as we lay in bed, full of anticipation for the demonstration we were going on the next day in Zagreb University, the demonstration that would call for our future to be recognised by Tito's government. I re-read Fisković's story as I finish my coffee.

This is an old story about the snow deer wedding. You might never have heard of such an animal, probably because they are very rare indeed, maybe a complete invention, but a Splićan believes in such a creature, just as much as he does the Mysteries of the Passion. It is said that the snow deer live in the Marjan Hill, hiding away from human contact. At the harshest time of the year, when the old year has barely spent its last breath, that's when a deer hunter might chance upon them. It's considered lucky to glimpse the deer, but unlucky to pick off one of their number. Why? Because they are the spirits of the dead; they are the spirits of those who have left this world too soon, because they were killed by another's hand, either deliberately, or in careless anger. There are always four deer at a wedding, and the reason is simple. One represents what has been, another the present. The remaining two speak of what is to be;

they are witness to the marriage of the past and the present; they will speak for each of the wronged spirits, bringing their names back to life, letting them carry on the winds and into the mountains and out to the seas. To kill one of the deer at this moment of union is to plunge the world back into turmoil and to destroy forever the possibility of reconciliation. So, if you see the snow deer, it is because something is about to be healed in your world. You must watch, wait, and allow enchantment to win out.

The story is signed by Antun Fisković and dated 28 October, 1971. I fold it back up into a neat little parcel and slot it back inside my purse. I know the story backwards; I have told and re-told it to myself down the years until I can visualise each and every detail just as Goran described them from viewing the painting in Fisković's studio. It was a night scene, he'd said, with snow lying heavy on the ground. The moon was shown escaping from a cloud overhead, revealing a pathway made up of the footprints of the snow deer that had criss-crossed each other's tracks, as if busy in conversation. This has been my private story for a long time and I have always kept faith with it because I wanted so much to believe that Goran's forgotten fate could be reversed; a miracle performed just like the one achieved in the wedding between the snow deer. The idea that Goran Petrić's name could be revived and celebrated seems like a distant chimera, but maybe now it can happen? Looking over my shoulder for a waiter, I catch sight of a huge poster advertising the retrospective of Fisković's work coming up next year, a poster promising *"unseen masterpieces that will revolutionise the understanding of this most misunderstood of Croatian artists."* Has the painting of "The Deer Wedding" survived and is it one of the *"unseen masterpieces?"* The thought stops me in my tracks.

Chapter 17
boat man
Hvar, July 1998

A week after the body is discovered on the islet off Hvar, I find myself in a bar on the piazza sharing a beer with Milica. It seems she's spent all her kuna on a guitar. I thought maybe some government agency gave her an allowance but she reveals that her landlord gave her the money. "To help me learn my music," she explains. Milica doesn't need a guitar to make her voice even more impressive. She plays by ear, plucking notes at random, but she's a gifted musician, far better than Josip or the members of his band.

It's midnight and the bar is lively. Milica plays quietly in one corner, but people are drawn to her playing. They move in closer and soon there's quite an audience. She's completely wrapped up in her song. I admire the way she can just shut the world out at will, although I wonder if she was taught by some brutal experience back on the frontline in Vukovar? A noisy coughing behind me interrupts my thoughts. I glance back and catch the eye of a young man standing about a metre away. He's probably near enough my own age, but has the kind of enviable self-contained look I can only aspire to. He wears threadbare jeans cut off below the knee and a small silver charm on a thin leather tie around his neck. He is dark-skinned with a silvery blond crew cut. He is fit and he's beautiful and he's staring at me like we're about to leap up and tango. I turn back to watch Milica, but I no longer hear the music, just my heart doing a strange kind of drumming.

"What's the name of the song, please?"

A voice close by, so close I feel another's breath against the nape of my neck. I don't need to turn round to know it's Tango Boy. I turn round. "I don't know. She just makes it up as she goes along." Which is what I must try and do with this stranger.

He smiles. "She's very good. Is she one of the theatricals?"

"She's in *The Tempest*. We both are."

"I hear you need a boat."

"Do I?" I realise he's talking about the company. Zdenka has been trying to source a fishing boat for use in the show, but without much luck. "And you have a boat?"

"Yes, I do."

I swivel round on my chair. I assumed he might be a student on holiday rather than a local. But that's just what he proves to be: the son of a fisherman from the island. Home on holiday from Siena University, but a bona fide man of the sea.

"I'm Kristijan, Kristijan Kovačić," he says, holding out his hand. We shake like businessmen, and he laughs. "Do I get your name by way of return?"

"I'm Dagmar Petrić."

He pulls up a chair and produces cigarettes and a lighter from a back pocket. We smoke and listen in companionable silence as Milica starts singing her song about the man with pearl eyes. The crowd whoops and hollers when she finishes. Kristijan asks me if she's recorded her songs and I fill him in on the little I know. He slides an arm along the back of my chair. Milica has packed up her guitar and is heading for the katamaran to take her back to Split. She barely acknowledges Kristijan when she leaves. He shrugs. The silver ankh on his leather necklace bounces against his collarbone and I'm tempted to still it. "Milica might not like meeting strangers," he says. "Maybe there have already been too many for her to deal with?"

I like it that he tries to understand her strangeness. I like it that he shakes my hand again when he drops me off at Hotel Lucic and then asks if I'd like to go for a drink after rehearsal one evening. "You can tell me why you need a boat for the show and I'll tell you why I need to charge an extravagant hire fee. We can maybe compromise. I'm open to offers."

Then he jumps down the steps leading up to the hotel, and disappears behind a tangle of palm trees. I see him again the day before I'm to visit Milica in Split. Kristijan offers to take me over on his boat. It will be a full day, because it's a three hour round trip to Split and back, but he suggests we make the most of it by walking in the Marjan Hill after my visit to my friend. I take up his offer without hesitation.

We meet at the harbour. A man sits at a little fold-out table outside the Post Office, sticking stamps on dozens of envelopes. He waves and wishes us a good trip. Kristijan nods in reply. He's a distant relation of some sort. "My family is like a huge fishing net. We seem to scoop up all sorts," he explains.

Kristijan is wearing his cut-off jeans and a loose white cotton shirt, unbuttoned with the cuffs turned back. He sweeps me through the shallows to his boat, tied up just a few metres from the harbour. It's a small fishing boat, but there's a cabin for shelter if the sun burns too hot. I opt to sit beside him, whilst he steers the boat out into the open sea. Very soon Hvar resembles a dried-up lump of broccoli. I climb out of the cabin and head towards the stern to count dolphins. Up ahead, the sea and the sky are both a luminous blue. I shield my eyes from the glare with my hand. Yes, there is something out there, a small dark shadow against the waves and then an arched back against the skyline. It is a dolphin. Kristijan is kneeling down at the side of the cabin, reaching his arm through the window to steer. He points straight ahead, without speaking. There's a second one, curving up against the sky with its partner in tow, like a duet. I hold my breath. Another dolphin rushes in from my left, a flash of fin passing so close I can hear it expel air through its blowhole in a soft "pssh". It is so close, it's almost under my feet.

The wind has picked up and is ruffling the water around the boat. Two dolphins plough through the water directly ahead, an older male with a set of distinctive markings on its fin and a younger male. They shift tack and gallop alongside us. Then they are still again, but close by. I've learnt to sense it now. I go back to the bow and see one of the males has popped up to ride fast behind us, as if giving chase. Kristijan points out another island off to our right, one where he swims naked, just off the rocks. He used to go and hunt on the island for gulls' eggs after Yugoslavian boats set up a blockade of Dalmatia during the recent war. "We couldn't fish; people were quite literally starving," he says, quietly.

Milica has drawn a diagram to help me find the way to her house. Kristijan knows Split very well, so offers to map read. We head for the Peristyle and take a sharp left away from Diocletian's Palace, into a narrow courtyard. Opposite stands a four-storey building with large wooden doors and a balcony along its entire length, decorated with coloured tiles. Stone lions prowl under the balcony and there are more creatures lurking under the roof. I double check the address on my piece of paper and then look back at the house. I can't imagine who might live in such a place – maybe some faded Party figure, or a minor Italian aristocrat and their family, left behind after the Second World War? Kristijan leaves me to explore and heads off to find some lunch in a bar at the harbour. I knock and Milica answers. She shows me into an enormous foyer, which I think could probably accommodate the whole of my Aunt and Uncle's apartment back in Zagreb. Its ceiling disappears into a mesh of spiders' webs illuminated by shafts of sunlight coming in through small stained glass panels sitting above large pillars. Beneath the webs, a black and white tiled floor rimmed with a border of contrasting blood red and crisp green lozenges. It's a stage set. We could perform *The Tempest* in the fireplace, except it's already occupied by a stack of neatly sawn logs.

Milica leads me up a flight of stone steps and into a narrow corridor. There is a very particular smell here, but I can't quite put a name to it, until she opens the door. Inside, there are dozens of easels and several trestle tables, all bearing evidence of an artist. I can smell oil paint and turps and the glue used on the stretchers. I'm disappointed to find there's no one at work. One particular painting catches my eye; I sense I've seen it before somewhere. It's large and rectangular: a forest of stylized trees beneath which roam four white deer. Each animal has been painted sideways on, but the eyes of each stare out directly at the viewer. Three of the deer have coloured pupils, and one has empty black ovals in place of its eyes. I kneel down and take in each carefully painted detail. I love the pattern of the tree branches – a thick, dark violet interspersed with a colour Milica describes as "viridian green". Even the paint names sound special. And then I remember where I've seen this painting before – or rather a small segment of it. Marko Strgar, the curator at Mimara Gallery, showed me one of the snow deer on his laptop.

"Is this Antun Fisković's studio?" I ask, hardly able to believe such luck.

Milica nods. "Yes. And this is one of his favourite paintings. He calls it "The Deer Wedding". It's based on a very old story from Dalmatia." She kneels down beside me. "You know, the snow deer are supposed to live on the Marjan Hill, not far from here. This is what Antun told me: when it snows heavily, so heavily it's like the world has been wrapped up in a sheet, that's when they come out. The snow deer marry and all is well with the world again. Antun's been working on this picture for over sixty years, not the same painting each time, but a different version of it."

"I think my father saw an early version when he came to Split in the Seventies," I tell Milica. I recall him mentioning snow deer on one of his tapes. Was this the painting he was going to tell my mother about on his return, or some story associated with it? I've got a lot more questions, but we're interrupted by the sound of a door being banged shut downstairs. A little later, the studio door swings open to reveal an old man, very stooped, with a mop of unkempt grey hair – I'm sure I can see flecks of paint in it – and milky white eyes, the colour of the deer skin. He wears a pair of baggy old trousers held up with a heavily ornamented belt and a thick blue denim shirt with a huge rip down its front. He's very wiry, which makes his hands look strangely too big for his wrists. The knuckles are prominent. It takes him a while to register our presence, but when he does, he lets out a huge roar. Milica starts to shake violently, and I rush over to hold her. She is hyperventilating. Fisković is shouting now: "What are you doing in here? Milica, this is an outrage. These are my private things and this bitch has not been invited."

Well, hello and nice to meet you too, Mr Artist. Milica is gulping down tears and her strangled breaths; I'm convinced she's going to choke, except help is at hand, at last. Someone else has followed Fisković into the atelier and takes control. It's Marko Strgar.

"Old man, shut the fuck up," he orders then walks over to Milica and gently strokes her shoulders until her breathing slows to a more steady pace.

Although I don't like Fisković's behaviour, I can't believe what Marko has just said. And isn't "Old Man" what Tito used to be called? People just don't use that expression, even ironically. Fisković stumps over to the easel, in case we've scribbled on it in biro like naughty schoolchildren. He leans in close, so close I think he might push it over with his beaky nose. "Did you touch it?" He looks at me with his pale ghost eyes. I shake my head. He steps up closer and stares harder still. I wonder if he might have lost his eyesight all together. He scans my face, but it's odd not seeing his eyes more clearly. Then I realise he's got cataracts over both of them, like two little cauls. He waves at me in a dismissive gesture. "Go, whoever you are."

Marko smiles reassurance. "Come, I'll show you the way." I look round for Milica, but she's already slipped out of the room. Marko guides me gently back to the foyer. "You mustn't mind the little scene back there," he says. "Antun is very guarded about his paintings. He doesn't want anyone to see them before the exhibition in Zagreb."

We are back in the tiled foyer and I glance up again at the cobweb ceiling. Marko follows my gaze. "Ah, centuries of history hang up there. Sometimes, you get calcified little insects falling on your head, like a special kind of snow. This place is a museum, a graveyard and an atelier all at once."

"How long will you be staying?"

"For as long as it takes."

I assume Marko is still making his selection for the exhibition. Fisković is evidently a difficult man to deal with, as well as the most surprising landlord I could imagine for poor Milica.

"I don't think he should have upset my friend, even if he is a famous artist," I venture.

"No, he shouldn't. But you know, he's probably already regretting what he did. He adores her. We both do." Marko opens up one of the big wooden entrance doors. "You're the first person Milica has invited here," he adds. "You must come back, really you must. Antun will be a pussy cat, trust me."

Can I trust Marko? He might well be here to keep an eye on Fisković and to stop Zdenka and myself from meeting him alone. And as for Milica, what if she never comes back to rehearsal? She might start shaking again so badly, she'll crumble up, like a desiccated winter leaf rubbed between my fingers. Marko takes my hand and plants a kiss on the back of it, an old-fashioned gesture but rather breathtaking all the same. "Of course I'll come back, if Milica wants me to," I reply, and walk out of Fisković's atelier in something of a daze.

Chapter 18
sheep shoes
Split, July 1998

Antun knew he was being unreasonable. To keep such a huge, rambling building to himself and a couple of handpicked companions. But it's what he'd always known. He'd never liked having too many people around. The best days had, ironically, been the harshest of days: Winter 1941, and Croatia at war. He slept in front of the atelier's fire, alongside Jakob and Tilde, all of them toasting their toes and dreaming away the days. A December as hard as any he had known. Ice sealed up the windows and petrified the ivy growing across the atelier's façade. It was colder inside the warehouse's huge, echoing chambers than it was outside. Ancient spiders' webs were made stiff as string in the frost that crept in through cracked sills and broken glass. The roof leaked and rainwater seeped into the rooms on each of the four floors. When it froze over, they found it a hazardous business crossing the terracotta and ornamental tiled floors. They stayed put for days at a time, whispering stories in puffs of frosty breath. There were days when Antun's fingers were so stiff with cold, he'd been unable to pick up chisel or mallet. Tilde made him a hat out of a piece of bear fur she'd found in the cellar. He had worn an old sheepskin jacket and waistcoat Branko had given him, under which he layered thin linen shirts and pages of newspaper in order to get a measure of extra warmth.

There had been no food, Antun remembered that most clearly. The harvest had failed and what little had been saved was sent overseas by the government to Germany. Branko was in the habit of stopping by from time to time with a fish wrapped in greaseproof paper, which Tilde cooked over the open fire and then shared out between the four of them. Branko was a smuggler, like many of the other fishermen from Hvar. He knew how to creep through the waves like a shark hunting its prey, a skill he had nurtured since the old Yugoslav government had hinted at bringing its economy in line with the New Economic Order of the Reich. Branko smuggled plum brandy and white wine past the

Kriegsmarine, and he smuggled people, like Jakob and Tilde, desperate to find a new life away from the alarming decrees being issued by the Ustaše government in Zagreb. Decrees that made Branko's love for Tilde impossible, because it had been forbidden for a Croat to marry a Jew. "I saw it with my own eyes," Branko told them one evening. "Pinned up outside the council chamber. But you tell me, how do you legislate against a man's heart?"

How indeed, Antun had often wondered. News of the decree had convinced Jakob of the need to flee to Ancona as soon as it was safe to do so – taking Tilde with him. Antun remembered her last kiss, blown up the stairs, soft as a seed head. He heard her crying even now, except it wasn't Tilde upstairs, but another refugee. Poor Milica from Vukovar. He'd shouted at her unnecessarily, and he should have just asked the stranger to leave, politely and quietly.

"You could have advised her to make an appointment at the Tourist Office, like everyone else," Marko had argued. "And no harm would have been done."

But he'd behaved like an ogre and made Milica cry. He sat listening to her, wrapped in his cloak and his bad temper. He shouldn't have shouted the place down, but who did this woman think she was anyway? Marko said she was another of the actresses from the island. Perish the thought. She might be a hostile critic, or a government employee checking up on him and his taxes. Marko had bristled when he'd asked him about money. "You think I'll spend your every last kuna, don't you?" Antun had denied this outright. Marko would make money out of him, for sure, but not by looking under his mattress.

He was worn out and too old to argue. But the real bombshell had exploded later in the evening when Marko brought him news about the discovery of a body. "A young woman's body, they say. She's been found on a scrap of land off Hvar." Antun hadn't needed a forensic scientist's report to convince him that it was Tilde's body which must have been dug up. And by whom? A property developer possibly, intent on building on the little island – a landing post for tourist boats, or a café, or some such newfangled idea. Little Tilde, dead and buried, her shroud sealed with lavender stalks and Branko's guilty kisses.

He'd retired to bed, claiming he felt unwell. Marko bid him good night and to remember to apologise to Milica in the morning. "Sleep on it, both of you. The world won't end overnight." But who could be sure of such a matter, Antun thought, shuffling up to his huge bed and clambering on it like a drowning man. He stretched out and felt the headboard under his fingertips. His feet barely made contact with the end of the bed. King of all he surveyed, which amounted to this: a threadbare canopy made out of a discoloured mosquito net; a carved wooden headboard and the tips of his toes in their soft leather slippers. He couldn't hear Milica crying anymore. Maybe she had fallen asleep? He turned on his side slowly. The thought of getting back up to remove his cloak and shirt was unendurable. He was exhausted. He had reached the end of a tunnel and found darkness, not daylight. There might be a simple explanation: he was dying. Antun clutched his heart, but it beat as loudly as it ever had. Strong as an ox, his doctor claimed, but he needed an operation on his eyes. He'd been stubborn and refused medical help for several years and suddenly he could barely see a smudge of colour in front of his nose. Marko knew people, of course, so an operation would be happening soon. He would see his way into his grave, at least.

Dear Jesus, but how many nights had he spent like this, wide-awake and fretting, listening to the cacophony inside the old warehouse. The whistling draughts and creaking roof beams; panes of glass rattling and banging at the frames like angry fists, and the slow, continuous drip of water through disintegrating plaster and rotten wood, coursing like so many tributaries, eager to find a way through the unfamiliar geography of tile and stucco. During the war years, hordes of rats had scampered late at night behind walls stained with mould, whilst a family of intrepid mice had taken up residence in an old sheepskin in the linen closet. Tilde ordered him not to set any traps. Up high in the attic, a nursery of bats swung with the winds, waiting for warmer days so they could fly through the broken roof tiles at dusk, curving a path round the lions. The bruising frosts of late winter had eroded the lion king's muzzle; its teeth had long gone and so had most of its once-impressive mane.

Antun had been kept busy carving headstones throughout that long, bitter January of 1942; he barely had time to keep up with his atelier's orders, let alone find time to rescue a Roman lion. The cold was so intense. Stone had been hard to come by, and the cost of importing it had risen, forcing Antun to slice up old dustsheets and stitch them into sketchbooks. He began drawing again, using thick black ink and a box of oil paints he found in a shop near the North Gateway. He mixed colours on squares of linen, stretched out between frames he made from fragments of wood shaved from packing cases.

Croatia was a country in her own right again – Nezavisna Država Hrvatska, a mint new Independent State of Croatia. Antun had heard the news announced on Zagreb Radio in a crowded harbourside bar. Branko was disappointed the Ustaše had come to power, largely because of the help of their Italian allies. Pavelić was the country's new leader, the Poglavnik. "Can it be this easy to make a new country, a new world?" Branko had demanded of Antun. "And what kind of independence means you give away your land to other countries, like parcels of cheese?"

Pavelić and his cronies had drawn up the frontiers of the new Croatia in a hotel in Vienna. Representatives from Germany and Italy had also been at the Imperial Hotel, each eager to play cartographer amongst the bone china coffee cups. It wasn't only Branko who was in despair. Since the declaration by the occupying powers the previous spring, Jakob had devised endless escape routes begging the man who loved his daughter to take them away from all they had ever known. Branko secretly met with Tilde in the cellars of the old warehouse, threading lilies and tiny peonies in her long dark hair and telling her stories about the old Dalmatia, the snow deer and their acts of enchantment, and the home he would build them on an islet a stone's throw from Hvar. "You can convert, become a Catholic and our problems are solved," he said. And Antun had comforted Tilde whose heart had turned cold as stone at such a plan. "I'm a Jew," she said. "This is who I am; I can no more change that than the world can do cartwheels round the moon. If this is what I am, why change me?"

Antun could still hear Tilde's remonstrations down the decades; it was as if the old warehouse sang its memories at such times, close to dawn, his eyes aching with lack of sleep. Glancing sideways, his better eye was caught by a thick band of light crossing the bedroom floor, getting wider. He half-raised his head, but he couldn't really see anything beyond the bright light.

"Antun?" His name just a whisper. Dear God, had his hearing disappeared too? Someone was beside the bed, but he could only see a shadow against the glow of light. An angel was stooping down and kissing his forehead. He was going to be bundled up like a baby and taken away. "It's me. I can't sleep." The voice was louder and he knew it to be Milica. She crawled on to the bed and he felt the mattress dip to one side. Antun remembered how she had talked in her troubled sleep when she first arrived in Split.

Back in her native Vukovar, Militisa had been crammed like a forbidden root into a cellar with a hundred strangers; praying for the bombing to cease and the ground to stop shaking under her bones; pushing up for air, her skin wet with sweat, with fear. Everyone else's fear stoppering up the cellar like a cork in a bottle. Milica shaking and praying and fighting for each breath in endless darkness. She had walked from Vukovar all the way to the coast, her feet bare and blackened with ash from destroyed houses and roads. Her hair and nails had grown to a spectacular length. She had dug roots up with her nails and wrapped her hair around her arms for warmth. She slept in holes in the ground; she slept between floorboards, wrapped in pieces of plastic sheeting. Sometimes, she found sheep's fleece caught on barbed wire, which she stuffed into some old shoes she'd found. Her nightmare was to wake up and find herself trapped in a hole, in total darkness, a strong wind blowing. No one else in sight, which meant safety on the one hand, unbearable loneliness on the other. Fear and solitude. These had been the two poles of her world.

"Stay," Antun said. "And I'll tell you about the girl they've found on the island."

What made him tell Milica about his half-sister, Antun had no idea. Maybe because she had been buried in a dark hole too? Poor Tilde. They thought she would be safe after she had been left behind on the flight to Ancona. A wounded Partisan had taken precedence, a chance act of fate brought to a terrible conclusion when the Kriegsmarine had caught up with the boat, just off Hvar. Jakob and a dozen other refugees had been shot and their bodies thrown overboard. Another notice pinned to the council's doors had warned of their fate.

"Will they unbury Tilde?" Milica asked, as Antun told her the story of Tilde and Branko's fated love from long ago. "Is that allowed?"

He knew it was, that there was a special word for taking a body up from the ground, but was it different if that place was unconsecrated? Besides, Tilde had been a Jew. Did that make a difference? He had no idea of the protocol in such matters, and hated himself for it. It was one more injustice for her.

"And they will put her back again, won't they, because she loved that place. And Branko will have joined her by now."

But Branko had died on some mysterious sabotage mission in the waters off Hvar, a year after the occupation. The first Partisan maritime patrol, and he was in command. Some brave undertaking, a handful of men, their faces blackened with dirt, knives between their teeth, explosives in their backpacks. Scuttling about like rats. No one really knew much more.

"I think he found her all the same," Milica insisted. "That little island is a place of magic, like in Shakespeare's play." She squeezed his hand. "You're crying, Old Man." She didn't sneer like Marko. She said the words with tenderness. He asked her to keep the story to herself. It still wasn't safe to say anything in public just yet. Milica agreed.

"I'm sorry," Antun said, as she shifted her pillows. "I'm sorry I shouted; I'm sorry I hurt you. And I'm sorry I'm not a better person, the kind of person who can really help you."

Milica was quiet. "Don't worry, Antun," she said eventually. "I've got my guitar and I've got a friend on the island. It's getting better, really it is."

"And you must ask her back, so I can apologise to her too. Will you do that?"

"Yes, I will. Her name's Dagmar."

"I'll ask Marko to buy cakes and we'll have a party."

"I can't remember much about parties."

"Don't worry. Marko can be master of ceremonies and keep Dagmar entertained."

Milica coiled up beside him. "I'll ask her when I'm next over at rehearsals. Marko has promised to sail over to Hvar soon."

Antun stayed awake, long after Milica had fallen asleep. She whimpered occasionally at a bad dream and once kicked out at his legs, but other than that she was quiet. He recalled her first night at the atelier, how she had found it impossible to give way to sleep. Marko had found her, lost and alone, sitting under a palm tree on Split harbour. He'd brought her to the atelier and she'd told them about living underground in a cellar for many months, and that her parents and her whole life had disappeared. She had sat on the floor, swaying with tiredness, determined to keep herself upright. Antun left her to go to bed, but tiptoed back in the early hours of morning and there she still was, biting her hands to keep herself from sleeping. She'd bitten her hands raw until Marko had finally intervened. "Enough is enough," he'd said. The first time she slept, it had been in Marko's arms. Antun wondered if he'd drugged her, or performed some kind of magic spell. Marko laughed off such suggestions. "I think she just wanted to be held. All those nights in the ground. She said she thought she might have died and turned into a ghost. She wanted to feel like a real person again, but had forgotten how. So I held her, that's all there was to it."

Chapter 19
jet coat blues
Hvar/Split, July 1998

A week after being ejected from Fisković's studio, I meet Milica on her way to rehearsal. She gives me a handmade envelope and, inside, I find a rough sketch of a snow deer and a short message, dictated to Milica by Fisković. He's asked me to come and stay for a few days by way of apology for his "unspeakable and uncivilised" behaviour. Milica promises he's repentant, but I don't need persuading. Rehearsals can wait – Zdenka still hasn't managed to persuade the island's dressmaker to make my bridal veil out of an old fishing net – and I'm owed overtime at Hotel Lučić. Kristijan thinks it might be an opportunity to find out more about Fisković's interviews with my father. He studies the sketch of the deer and manages to work out the signature and the date: August, 1946. "It's really old, Dagmar. Maybe you can sell it and pay for your art course?"

I think it's a talisman for future discoveries, so ignore Kristijan's advice. I take the katamaran over to Split at the weekend and discover that Fisković really is a changed man. He welcomes me in person, leading me up the stairs and apologising several times. "I have so few visitors, but it's hardly a surprise when I behave like such an oaf. You must forgive me. You must blame my advanced years."

Fisković is certainly an old man; he walks carefully up each step, gripping the banister as he goes. When we turn the corner, he almost topples over. I steady him as best I can. He laughs good-naturedly, but I think it's a false laugh, because he doesn't like being dependant on anyone. Inside the atelier, a small feast has been laid out on a trestle table under the balcony windows. There are bottles of wine, bottles of Jamnica water, a jug of orange juice with a small beaded mesh cover, plates of fish and big bowls of salad. Smaller dishes contain little floating candles shaped like flowers. Marko is playing waiter. He piles food onto a plate and hands it over with a flourish. I wonder if he's ever been an actor. Milica sits at the other end of the table, nibbling at a small dish of olives. She eats like a bird, whatever the temptations before her.

"*Scarcity and want shall shun you,*" Fisković says, leading me up to the table.

It's a quote from *The Tempest*. I'm not sure if I should mention that our director Eos has abandoned Prospero's fantasy banquet in favour of a wrestling match between the spirit world and the shipwrecked crew. The idea, according to Zdenka, is that this will represent the primacy of truth over pretence and lies, a much-needed axiom in our post-war times. I think I'd prefer a banquet, all the same. Looking round the atelier, I see the canvas "The Deer Wedding" has been moved towards the fireplace. I walk over to take another look. Marko follows.

"There are only a handful of preparatory sketches for this work," he says, catching up with me. "Antun didn't always have money for paper, so he had to draw on the floor. Just imagine what these floorboards could tell us, if we had some of that special forensic powder, you know, the kind that shows up bloodstains years after a murder."

I stare down at the floorboards and, just as if I were really party to Prospero's magic, I believe I can see a riot of ghostly deer and spindly trees beneath my feet. I look back up at the painting. It's different, but I don't immediately spot what's changed. When I do, I'm surprised. Fisković has painted a pair of eyes on the fourth deer, the one at the tail end of the little procession. This wouldn't be such a shock, except he has painted *my* eyes.

"You've guessed right," Marko says, leaning in so close I can smell the soap on his skin. "Fisković thinks your eyes are the future."

"But I've got nothing to do with this story."

"In some ways, you've become the story, Dagmar."

Marko wanders off, satisfied that an explanation has been made, but I'm confused. Why has Fisković done this – and how? He's practically blind with cataracts, but he's caught their shape really well. Milica explains when she joins me. She described the shape of my eyes to Fisković and guided his paintbrush. She also helped him mix the exact right shade of green. I feel betrayed, which is ridiculous. Milica wouldn't want to offend me, surely? I wonder if I'm being selfish and ungrateful. Lots of people would jump at the chance to be put into a painting. I'm reminded uncomfortably of another gesture, one Aunty Rozana made when I was thirteen. I'd seen a beautiful coat in one of my mother's *Neu Style* magazines, designed by Jean Paul Gaultier. It was a tailored denim coat, decorated with hundreds of jet beads and a raven feather collar. I'd wanted the coat for my birthday.

"And where in the name of God and the Holy Apostles would you wear such a thing?" Aunty Rozana had mocked. The coat became a symbol of everything I most wanted but was out of my reach; my mother; a social life of unremitting glamour and a future made up of exotic things that were absent from our crowded, rented apartment where I was reduced to wearing second-hand plastic shoes because leather cost. One day, I would buy shoes for hundreds of pounds, just like the ones in the magazines; outlandish, impractical shoes which fitted my feet to perfection. No more blisters or corns. Aunty Rozana had spent night after night making me a replica of the coat, but it was a travesty to my selfish teenage eyes. She made her coat out of old jeans and plastic sequins, and I refused to wear it. I hadn't known at the time that it had been lovingly crafted over many long nights following weary hours cleaning factory floors.

The guilt I felt about that coat is what I feel now. Somehow, I know I'm in the wrong again. I leave the atelier and head down the stairs, directionless but unable to stay in the studio whilst I feel so angry. I stop in the middle of the tiled hall, conscious someone has followed me out. It's Milica. She stands at a safe distance, her arms loose by her sides, as she always does in rehearsal when there's any outburst of real emotion. "Antun didn't want to upset you. I know he didn't. He just thought your eyes were right. Maybe he should have asked you first, but I don't think that's what artists do, do they?"

I've no idea, either. Milica sits down on the bench in front of the fireplace. She looks like a sparrow against its huge stone surround. I sit next to her and dry my eyes on the back of my hand. I tell her about Aunty Rozana's coat.

"Parents know we will be disappointed, so they try and teach us that as soon as they can," Milica says. "Mama said not to trust the paramilitaries. Our neighbours waved to them when they played cards outside the bars, but not Mama. She wouldn't sleep with one of them and they shot her. I don't know his name. I don't suppose she knew it, either. She was shot by a Serb, even though she was a Serb. I think she knew what would happen. She kept me safe by warning me."

I feel ashamed all over again. My stupid dream of a fabulous coat compared to Milica's trauma of losing her mother. We're interrupted by a loud knocking at the door and find Kristijan outside on the step. He looks sheepish, claims he was "just passing by" and asks if I'd like to go for a walk. Milica smiles at him this time, even runs back upstairs to gather up some fruit and bottles of water for our trip. I follow Kristijan back out into the crowded Peristyle. He weaves through the café tables and chairs with the easy authority of someone who has soaked up knowledge like sand through his toes. We walk in near silence through streets dazed with the early afternoon heat. As we move beyond the city walls, we find ourselves climbing up a winding track. Soon, we've reached a tiny stone chapel looking out to sea.

"It was probably a stop-over for pilgrims," Kristijan says.

We share apples sitting on a bench close to the chapel. It feels like we've walked into a parallel world of stone and silence. A butterfly lands on Kristijan's forearm and rests there. It's orange and red with big white spots. I'm not sure why I need to mention Josip, but I do. He listens with no expression to my garbled account of life with the Rock Star. His eyes are creased up against the intense glare. The butterfly has stayed put, like a very ornate tattoo. "So, I'm thinking of calling it a day," I continue. "But I should do it face to face. I think that's only fair."

"Why?"

"Why what?"

"Why does it make it fairer if you say it to his face and not over the phone? I've never really got that. It's shit either way, if you still care."

"But he doesn't, Kristijan. It's taken me a while to realise it, but I think he'd miss Dunk if he left the band more than he'll ever miss me. And he hates him most of the time."

"All the best bands are about rivalry. Look at The Fall."

Kristijan sits back on the bench and slips one arm over towards me. I lean into his sun-hot skin and try not to puzzle too much over the luck that has come my way since leaving Zagreb. The chance encounter with Fisković, discovering "The Deer Wedding" – being *in* "The Deer Wedding" – and now Kristijan too. He doesn't seem to pose, or get caught up in any petty rivalries. He just seems to take what comes with an easy forbearance. We both get up at the same time and continue our journey. The intimacy that has grown up between us in this short space of time feels as natural as the stones of the chapel walls. Up and up we go. There are wide stone steps set into the ground to ease our way. Several athletes are using these for track training purposes, some with coaches, others pounding up and down their length on their own, checking their stopwatches. Close to the top, we come to a sign announcing Marjan Zoo.

The spell cast on us is shattered within minutes of entering. It's a place of almost unimaginable ugliness and cruelty. The bare cages, some of which are exposed to the cruel sun, are little better than open-air dungeons for the wild beasts that pace desperately up and down. A brown bear sits slumped in a cage which is woefully inadequate for his furry bulk. Our eyes meet through the mesh. He seems to slump down even further into his skin. Past the bear's cage, a small herd of deer stands listless and shabby in a pen that has no vegetation to graze on – unless you count the dry stalks of weeds pushing through the cracked cement. I remember Fisković's painting of the snow deer and wonder that these scraggy creatures might be of the same stock. Close to tears, I slip my hand into Kristijan's. Neither of us speaks as we make our way through the zoo.

"We should make a complaint," I say eventually. "You can't keep animals in such conditions."

"I've never seen the point of zoos," Kristijan replies. "Either an animal fends for itself in the wild, or it dies. That's just nature."

"And this is a freak show."

Kristijan squeezes my hand. "Who will you complain to?"

I've no idea, which makes me feel even more inadequate. We start our walk back to the city, Kristijan doing his best to console me. He suggests we talk to the council, or write a letter to a government minister. My sandals have rubbed my feet, so I take them off, but the stone steps leading down to the city are too hot to stand on. Kristijan ends up giving me a piggyback. Once we're back in civilisation, we find a café overlooking the sea. A waitress serves us lemonade and hunts out some plasters for my blisters. Kristijan rolls a cigarette in his calm, measured way and lets me share it. Each time we swap over the cigarette, we kiss. Long, slow kisses. Walking away from the café, we come across a tumbled-down pair of gates at the top of a small bank. The gates are chained together, but there are huge gaps either side, easy enough for us to slip through. We find ourselves in a cemetery, but it's long been abandoned. The headstones have eroded, or they lie slip-shod on top of their graves. The lettering on them is a mystery. It's not Serbian, Croatian, Latin or Italian.

"I think it's Hebrew," Kristijan says. "My father told me there was a Jewish cemetery in Split. This must be it."

"Does anyone still come here, do you think?"

"I doubt it. There's so much else to repair after the war, who cares about an old cemetery where no one comes to pray anymore." Kristijan kneels down to knock pinecones off one of the few undamaged headstones. I crane over his bowed back to read the name as it comes back into sight:

Hepzibah Eschenasi
N. 28.6.1902.
M. 22.7. 1936

The name intrigues me. Wasn't Antun Fisković the son of Jakob Eschenasi, a merchant of Split? And could this have been the wife he cheated on? I feel a stab of excitement, after all the unpleasantness of the trip to the zoo. Kristijan gets back up and, taking my hand, leads me back down the slope to the lop-sided gates. The cicadas' incessant chattering is the only sound in the baking lunchtime air. Kristijan lifts me over the collapsed wall and down onto the street. "I'm sorry, Dagmar. It's not been much of a day has it? Distressed animals and ruined graves."

I know what he means, but another part of me is happy that I've shared these things with him all the same – and that I've maybe found another link to the story my father unearthed on his visit to Dalmatia. Kristijan pulls my hair back from my face and kisses me hard on the mouth.

Chapter 20
the heart of the matter
Split, July 1998

Dagmar had been to the Jewish Cemetery and seen Hepzibah's grave. Marko told Antun the news when he had returned from Mass. He also revealed she was Goran Petrić's daughter. "You remember him, don't you? The Maspok journalist who wanted to make you headline news?" Antun remembered an intense young man with the most extraordinarily expressive face and beautiful long hands, like those of the concert pianist Horowitz; fingers like floating tendrils which he'd longed to paint, though he'd been shy of asking. The tapes recording their interviews had, apparently, survived all this time, but the man with the tendril-fingers and the love of words had died. "Took his own life, Old Man. Strung himself up, like a bunch of onions."

"What does she know, exactly?" Antun interrupted.

Marko shrugged. "Everything and nothing. But I would love to hear those tapes."

Antun shared his sentiment, but for different reasons. Marko was in charge of the retrospective and probably thought the tapes would help him with his background research, but Antun wanted to listen and remember the clever young man who had winkled him out of his shell. His interview technique had been instructive. Petrić had the gift of inciting others with his enthuasiasm for life and its possibilities; even in the drab era in which he'd been raised. He'd shone out of the failed Communist regime like a shiny coin spinning on a dull pavement. He'd told Petrić about the paintings. He'd shown him "The Deer Wedding" and explained its history. He'd even admitted a young Jewish girl was the sitter for "A Portrait of Croatian Womanhood". No, he'd gone further than that. He'd admitted the girl was his half-sister, Tilde Eschenasi. Marko slammed into his memories, thrusting a sketchbook into his hands.

"See if you can date this," he demanded. "I think they are

costume drawings from *The Tempest*. I'm going out, but try and do this before I get back. We're behind schedule, Old Man."

Poor Marko and his endless schedules and deadlines. Antun nodded acquiesance, but had let the sketchbook slip from his knees the minute the curator left. He found it hard trying to work out the scribbles and sketches in his old books. Sometimes, his tired eyes could only see shapes and he had to try and imagine the rest. He dozed off, but was woken by an unfamiliar footfall. Antun waited to hear a voice he could properly identify. There was a prolonged silence.

"Are you awake, Mr Fisković?"

Antun struggled to place the voice in the dark room, then realised it was Dagmar. She was his guest for the weekend, of course, but he'd thought she was out with Milica on a picnic to the Marjan Hill that had been talked about, or with her young man. They'd not spoken since she'd left in a temper. Milica had claimed it was because he'd used her eyes without permission in his painting; he felt concern at upsetting her all over again. But an artist always borrows and rarely asks, surely? Antun tried to remember how he had approached the fisherwomen of yesteryear. He'd often sat sketching them without their even noticing his arrival or departure. He'd become part of the backdrop, an extension of the harbour wall. Antun smiled a wry smile. He'd blended in for once in his life.

"I'm glad you've come back," he said, turning in what he assumed was Dagmar's direction. He cocked an ear and waited for the slightest of sounds that might give away her actions. There was nothing. He wondered if she might be holding her breath. "I don't have time to explain myself these days. I'm sorry if I'm clumsy about it. Once upon a time it was different, but now, the world passes me by." A whisper of fabric, maybe a skirt rustling against knees, or a sleeve pushed up over an elbow? Antun turned right round and faced the direction of the door. There was a dark smudge just beside it, which he took to be Dagmar. "I asked Milica to help me. It wasn't her idea. Can you understand?"

"I think so."

Her voice sounded tearful, too soft. She was still upset. Antun struggled with his words, anxious to catch the right tone. Milica had talked a lot about Dagmar at the rehearsals on the island and he'd liked what he'd heard. "I wanted quite literally, I suppose, to find a fresh pair of eyes for my painting. The eyes of a new generation."

Antun sensed the dark shape move forwards. Dagmar's sandals made a distinctive squeaking sound as she walked. He waited, before speaking again. A hand lightly touched his arm. "I'm not angry, Mr Fisković, just a bit confused."

"A Splićan would know at once what this is all about." Antun gestured towards the canvas that now stood behind him. "The story is very old, but it never loses its magic – or its importance. I've lived a lot longer than you and I've seen the world spin round any number of times. History repeats, and so it's vital the snow deer are not thrown off course, either. The wedding is symbolic, of course. It's all about the need for reconciliation, for the lost to be found, and for that story and meaning to be passed on."

"I went to the Jewish cemetery yesterday. The graves there are all ruined, so there's nothing to pass on."

"Was it damaged at all?"

"No, not really, just rotting away. Maybe there are no relatives left to come and leave flowers, or tidy up."

Antun hesitated. Dagmar was testing him, just like her father had done before her. The seemingly casual mention of the cemetery. Marko had warned him: she knew things about his past. But the question was, what didn't she yet know? Antun made his way to his chair and sat down. He asked Dagmar to join him. She pulled up a chair opposite. If he leant forwards, he could see her outline; if he really craned forwards, he might see the green of her eyes. "You gave me the chance to finish my painting, now I must give you a gift in return," he said. Beside his chair, there was a small velvet box. He asked Dagmar to open it. Inside, was the Fortuny dress Tilde had worn long ago, dancing in the atelier on the eve of what they all thought might be a brand new world.

The same cornflower blue Fortuny dress his mother had worn when she had appeared in the theatre on Hvar island, the year before the First World War broke out; the year she had fallen in love with the merchant Jakob Eschenasi. The dress was one of Fortuny's famous

Delphos dresses, based on the pleated chitons worn by Greek women thousands of years ago. It slipped through the fingers like a worried leaf, only the strips of glass Venetian beads on its shoulders keeping it from falling at the wearer's feet. *"Faithfully antique, but powerfully original"* was the French writer Proust's verdict on such a dress. Jakob had given the dress to Elenora; she had returned it when their affair had come to its sad close, writing in one of her letters that his daughter Tilde was to wear it when she came of age. He had read about the dress in one of the letters Jakob had handed him the night he had revealed he was his real father.

"I hope you like it," he said to Dagmar. "It might even be a suitable costume for Miranda to wear."

She held the dress against her. He saw a blurry waterfall in front of him, as the blue silk cascaded to the floor.

"It's so beautiful," she half-whispered.

"This dress has always made people catch their breath. And its wearer."

"But surely it's too valuable to wear to the beach? That's where we're going to be performing."

"Your choice. But either way, the dress is yours. A gift from an artist who thanks you with all his heart for what you have done for him."

"I didn't really do anything though."

"Ah, some of the impressions we make on people we never really understand. Sometimes, that is a sad thing, but sometimes, it's a blessing."

Dagmar sat back down. She leant in closer. He could smell her scent, a rich mix of lime and cedarwood. "What impression did you have of my father, Goran Petrić?"

Antun thought he would be ready for Dagmar's question, but still it made him flinch. He hadn't known his mother, not really, and that fact had gnawed away at his heart over the years. Dagmar had shared such pain, but what could he do to bridge the years between father and daughter? He recalled that Petrić had come to the atelier on half-a-dozen visits, possibly more. Each time, they had talked, looked at paintings, drunk thick black coffee and shared cigarettes. Petrić had been eager to hear all Antun's stories; he'd wanted to hear them spoken in the old dialect of the islands, čakavski. Antun had felt like a small, weak root finally breaking through a crust of frosty soil in the younger man's company. He'd reminisced about the island of his birth and how it had shaped his love of the sea and the coast.

"Hvar is rich in history, even if its people are poor," he now explained, in turn, to Goran's daughter. "This is what I told your father, even though he'd been a city boy all his life. I told him how the islanders live, pressed close together like the skins of an onion. They know the sea's moods as closely as they do those of the lover or child who sleeps beside them. Everyone knows everyone else and knowledge is stored, like precious flour in a stone jar." Even the dead were never forgotten, he continued, a silent mass that never really grew old or left the island. Nor did the island's many exiles stay absent, the men and women who had disappeared when its Venetian occupiers bled the land dry over the centuries, taxing salt and letting fish rot in men's hands, even as the sea threw up more catches to those same men, thin as prisoners. "They are still spoken about in their mother tongue, in the little alleys leading away from the harbour," Fisković added. "For far too long, the islanders have had to speak and pray in a foreign language; too many words and stories still lie buried, deep as bones."

Dagmar touched his arm, gently. "Mr Fisković, I have a letter your mother wrote to you, but never sent. I know about her and your real father Jakob Eschenasi. I think my father knew all about it too. He wanted to write your story, but he was stopped. At least, I think that's what happened."

"You mustn't fall into the same trap as your father, Dagmar."

"What do you mean?"

"No one can expect to be the conscience of the Croatian nation. He tried to delegate the job to me, of all people."

"Why?"

"Maybe he felt sorry for me."

"I've listened to tapes he made of your interviews together. He admired you, I know it."

"He was young and impressionable."

"I don't think you believe that. My father was convinced Croatia's culture and economy could be revived; he saw your survival as a measure of what couldn't be destroyed."

Antun struggled with the tears that were threatening. Memories of his fireside debates with Petrić got jumbled up with earlier memories of Tilde and Jakob grilling fish over the fire's flames, Branko stalking the perimeter of their little circle, arguing with himself, if no one else cared to, over some political setback. "So much was lost," he said, his voice choking on the last word. Dagmar was still holding his arm. She tightened her grip. He was surprised at the strength in her. "What happened to them, Mr Fisković? The Eschenasis, I mean. I only found Hepzibah's grave. Was she Jakob's wife? Was she the reason Elenora couldn't marry?"

"Yes, she was Jakob's wife." He paused. "Jakob loved this place and he knew it better than any of us, its history, its stories, its very pulse. I was privileged to know this man."

"What happened to him?"

"He was killed trying to escape to Ancona."

"I see."

"Do you? I wonder. You know, this was once Jakob's warehouse. I bought it from him so he would have the money to pay for his passage. The only rotten bargain he ever made in his life."

"And he taught you about Split's history?"

"An outsider is sometimes the best judge, don't you think?"

"It's how you're being judged by people like Marko Strgar."

"It's a cliché, the artist rebel."

"You don't think you fit that description."

"Dear God, I'm a crab in its shell, not a fool on a barricade."

"Marko tells me there has been a call from the government to return your public statues to their pedestals. Like the War Memorial that used to be here, in the harbour. The one of Branko Ostojić, the Partisan hero. You knew him, didn't you?"

The introduction of Branko's name into the conversation worried Antun. Another chance remark on Dagmar's part? He struggled to think of a way of avoiding answering, but thankfully was rescued by his curator's arrival. Marko had quickly ejected Dagmar from her seat.

129

"You can talk again at lunchtime," he promised, escorting her back out of the atelier. He was less circumspect on his return. "You okay, Old Man? She's far too close to things, isn't she?"

"Afraid she'll steal your thunder?"

Antun smiled to himself. Marko wasn't happy about Dagmar's arrival, nor did he like the fact that she wouldn't let him borrow her father's tapes. "I mean, what use can she make of them?" he'd asked. Antun wondered. Was she maybe planning to finish what her father had started all those years ago? Marko hovered by his chair, waiting for Antun to acknowledge him again. "The newspapers are making quite a story out of that body found near the island. They're saying it's a woman's body, and that it was probably buried over fifty years ago."

"Nothing else?"

"No. She's been a long time dead. Maybe there's nothing else to know."

Antun looked up at Marko with his half-blind eyes. "You and I both know that's not true."

Chapter 21
Elenora's letter
Split, July 1998

Zdenka rings me on my mobile, anxious to know how I'm progressing with Fisković. She handed me a list of questions before I came over to the mainland, but I explain he's proving very evasive and I haven't yet had a chance to ask any of them. I've also been distracted by Milica who has been keen to show me round the warehouse and explore some of the ice cream parlours and cafés close by.

"Hell's teeth, Dagmar. You're the daughter of two investigative journalists," Zdenka snaps.

"But Marko's always lurking about. I'm surprised he doesn't just gag Antun and be done with it."

"Can't you get Kristijan to abduct him?"

My cousin would, no doubt, organise just such a scheme, but I'm not so devious. "Look, Zdenka, I'll give it one more try, but I'm leaving tonight…."

"Just get him to read the letter Vesna gave me. See what his reaction is."

Zdenka hangs up and I sit back down on my bed. My bedroom is on the second floor of the warehouse, just above the battered lion's head on the balcony. Sparrows wash themselves in the guttering that runs over my bedroom window, and I'm sure there are rats or mice scuttling overhead at night. But the room itself is all faded magnificence. I love the intricately carved wood stove in one corner and its tiled surround. Each tile has a different painting, telling an old nursery rhyme. It's a room for a child, but Fisković has never had any children, which is sad. That thought prompts me to pick up my file, including a photocopy of Elenora's letter, and head back downstairs. It's four o'clock in the afternoon, so Fisković might well be having a siesta. Although he can't see well enough to paint or draw, he still likes going to his studio each day to talk through his portfolios and sketchbooks with Marko. I heard Milica go out with Marko earlier to buy some new guitar strings, so there's a small chance I might be able to talk with Fisković undisturbed.

I push open the atelier door. Fisković sits on his chair, close to the painting of "The Deer Wedding". He wears a tatty old robe, decorated with little bits of mirror. Its faded lining features little embroidered hammers and sickles. He explained the other day that it's an old stage costume. It was made for a production of *The Tempest*, staged on Hvar in 1942 by Dalmatia's Italian occupiers. Antun had rescued Prospero's cloak after the first night descended into chaos with a Partisan raid on the mainland resulting in the majority of the audience disappearing to fight off the attackers. Antun hears me at the door. "Dagmar? Is that you?"

"I was running through some lines for my show and wondered if you'd help me, Mr Fisković."

It's only a small lie, but he accepts it and waves me in to the atelier. Late July, and the intense heat lingers. Even with the windows flung open on the balcony and the doors propped with folded pieces of cardboard, I feel as though my skin is slipping from my bones. I sit down on a stool beside Fisković's chair and pull out Elenora's letter. He waits, expectantly.

"Actually, there's something else I'd like to read to you first, if you don't mind. It's a letter written by your mother, one my cousin Zdenka was given by an actress who knew her. She was called Vesna Skurjeni."

A long pause. Fisković sits immobile, almost as though he's one of his own carvings. His large face, with its swept back mane of grey hair, is as imposing as the lion's head on the facade of his house, although both have been ravaged by the passing years. He rests his hand on my shoulder. "Yes, you can read it to me, Dagmar. Keep reading, and don't stop until you reach the end."

I follow his advice. The letter begins with Elenora explaining that she's writing by candlelight in a room once rented by her son, the one she gave away at birth and tried desperately to contact – without success – when he came to study fine art in Zagreb as a young man. A room where she cherishes a curl of dark hair he has left behind, snagged in a cheap comb, and a sliver of almond scented soap he once used.

She moves on to talk about her love affair with Jakob, conducted in the cellars of a warehouse filled with treasures from the world over; his wife Hepzibah lying in a room high under the rafters, sick and grieving for a son, stillborn just eighteen months previously.

Did I feel guilt, or horror at what I was doing? Elenora writes. *To my shame, I have to admit I did not. During the intense heat of long, slow afternoons, I was hungry only for this singular man, a hunger made bearable when I stepped down into the cold cellar and made love to him.*

The island of Hvar had welcomed Elenora as a young actress; she'd been cast as The Spirit of Serb-Croat Coalition in a pageant staged in 1913 in protest at those who would see Slav fight against Slav. A year later, the island had hidden her when she gave birth to her illegitimate son. Jakob had arranged for a friend to take her in, Dragutin Ostojić, a local fisherman. His wife Viktorija perfumed her sheets with lavender, grown all over the island, thick as a carpet; and she'd rubbed her aching, twitching legs with ice cubes.

Viktorij sang you into the world, Antun. She sang again when Jakob picked you up and cradled you in his arms. He held your cheek against his own and smiled in wonderment. Voices in the room next door called out blessings; our Lady was paraded through the small house, her white oval face gleaming inside a gilt picture frame; Fisković, the pretend father, rubbed my hands between his tool-scarred hands and promised a future for my son, his son. Words got tangled up, like fish in a net. He laughed at his hopes, and toasted Jakob who it was once believed rescued you from a storm. Then he joined the men in the room beyond to drink plum brandy and sing in the first morning of your bright future. Starlight lit up your face, the first night I held you; the only night I held you. Jakob crept in at dawn and took you, whilst I slept. Viktorija told him it was for the best, because you would only wake and cry if you smelt milk on me.

Jakob had stayed with Hepzibah, Elenora had returned to Zagreb. Her new playwright lover had to howl down her adversaries from the theatre stalls when angry protests broke out against the National Theatre for daring to hire a Serb actress. Elenora had been nearly destitute, forced to share a bed in cheap lodging houses with her friend

Vesna. Although Elenora was an actress, she couldn't play the role she most longed to play, the role of belonging in the city where she had been born and brought up.

I only survived, she reveals in her letter, *because for a time Jakob sent me money and strangers offered quiet gestures of support, like the man who cooked palačinke near my room in Ilica. He let me warm my fingers in the ashes from his oven, offered them to me on the tip of his shovel. "It's not right," he said. "You were my dream once. I don't like to think of you down here on the streets like us, cold and alone." His pity wasn't deserved. He didn't know I'd given you away, my only child.*

I stop at this point, because I can't help myself. Elenora's words evoke another memory, but this one is my memory. The day my mother left Zagreb for good, or so she told Uncle Darko and Aunty Rozana. I wasn't supposed to hear, but I'd hidden myself behind the sofa in their living room. "This city has never been my home," she'd said. "There's nothing left for me here."

"Dagmar? Has the letter finished?"

Fisković's hand finds my shoulder again and gives it a gentle squeeze. He's sensed something is wrong, but isn't sure what. I find my place and start reading again. I hadn't thought about it for months, not even with my mother appearing out of the blue, and our rather blundering attempt at reconciliation. Did Ana feel the same way as Elenora when she returned to Slovenia? And did she ever write me such a letter? Elenora's grief at losing her son so evidently dominated her life, in many ways it shaped it. She never stopped thinking about Antun, nor did she give up hope of him recognising her at the life drawing classes where she worked as a model and her son was a star pupil of the great Croat sculptor Ivan Meštrović. But Antun had never been told the story of his birthright, because the letter had never been sent. Antun was also a friend of Milan Gregorević, a man Elenora identifies in her letter as Ustaša. I glance up at Fisković, but his face is impassive.

It was when I saw you at the corso that I saw the danger you were in, the danger of being captured by one so brilliant, with his angel eyes and cruel, red mouth, Elenora's letter continues. *Vain and deluded, sporting a green velvet frock coat, spats and a fancy hat. And you holding on to his shoulder, as if a wind were sweeping you away from his wretched words. Antun, words sung you into this world; but the likes of Gregorević would never guess that. He kills and maims; he lives to create division and despair.*

Elenora ends her letter begging her son to reach her via Rabuzin, her playwright lover. It is dated 1936. "She never sent it, according to Vesna, because she realised it would be too dangerous if it were ever read by anyone except yourself."

"Her logic was sound, Dagmar, even though it went against her instincts. I learnt how to live like this myself, even without reading her letter."

"You mean, you could never have told your friend Milan about your adoption?"

Fisković laughs, but it's a tense, jarring kind of laugh. "No, of course I couldn't have told him, had I known then what I do now. But you know, I was never his brother in arms. I was never an Ustaša. Our relationship wasn't based on politics."

He looks down at me with his shrouded eyes, trying to gauge my expression, but I must look like the faint disc of a moon trying to shine through a late afternoon sky.

"We were close, Dagmar, but not allies. Too close, for the times we lived in, if you understand."

Fisković and Milan were lovers. I take a minute or two to absorb that. Fisković tells me of encounters in quiet streets that ended in hard blows; his body cut and broken up like an old plate. He loved men, not women, at a time when this alone could have led to his social ostracisation. He loved men like Milan who hit and punched him as if he were a stupid dog. "I had no pride, no shame, just this overwhelming love, and it nearly killed me."

His story shocks me, because it makes me understand more clearly why he's had to live in his self-imposed exile all these years. He's no more Ustaša than my father and his fellow reformers were; he's a man who has been forced to be a secret even to himself, because of prejudice. Fisković adds that Marko knows all about Milan and the affairs with his workshop assistants in the past; he's working quietly behind the scenes to ensure such information isn't misrepresented when the retrospective yields what the artist himself calls "bloody home truths". What more can anyone do to me, after all?" he asks. "Besides, I might not live long enough to see the exhibition open."

I remember Zdenka's list of questions at this point, but another thought occurs to me and I abandon her list again. "Was Branko related to the Ostojićs who helped your mother when she was pregnant?"

"Yes, he was their son."

"And they knew the Eschenasis?"

"Of course. Jakob was a good friend to many of the islanders. He found work for those who fell on hard times. And he helped keep the theatre on the island open. He donated bolts of cloth for the costumes and paid for the gilt paint on the boxes and chairs in the auditorium."

"Did Branko know your story?"

"Not exactly. It was felt best to let only a few people in on my secret. When Branko joined the Partisans, it might have put him at risk. If he had known such things, many innocent people might have suffered. My world has always been a complicated one, Dagmar. I kept on the right side of the Italian occupiers, because it was a useful way of keeping them from investigating people like Branko."

"You were a spy?"

Fisković laughs, but it's not such a hollow laugh as before. He's genuinely amused by the idea. "I don't think I can be given such a grand title. I told lies now and then, and I designed costumes for Marco Fuesli's production of *The Tempest*. Fuesli was the Italian military chief's translator at Split council. He turned a blind eye to some of the illegal trading taking place off the coast in return for association with a great artist such as myself."

"Were you at the theatre when the raid happened?"

"I was standing in the wings, waiting to go on as Trinculo." Fisković tries to sound flippant, but his manner has changed. He's edgy now, as if anxious to steer clear of something. "You know, over fifty years have passed since then, Dagmar. My memory is as ragged as my cloak."

He smoothes down his robe and settles back in his chair, as if ready for sleep. I don't want to stop our conversation yet. I feel I'm about to learn about the real heart of the matter, in spite of what he's just revealed about his love affair with Gregorević. I'm on the verge of putting Elenora's questions to Fisković when Marko, as if on cue, steps into the atelier. He's ready to take me back to Hvar on his boat and shoos me back up to my room to pack. I ring Zdenka and tell her to expect me about eleven o'clock at Hotel Lučić. She wants to know there and then what I've found out, but I stall her.

"Okay, okay. Later it is. But I've got news for you, as it happens. Your mother's just turned up."

"What?"

Although we've been in regular contact by mobile since she went back to Ljubljana, she hasn't once mentioned coming to Hvar. We last spoke three days ago and she was still worrying over her endlessly postponed television interview with Tudman. She hadn't even asked after rehearsals.

"Large as life, and twice as demanding," Zdenka hisses. "Get back as soon as. Your cousin needs you."

Chapter 22
lemon house
Hvar, July 1998

Marko had taken Antun over to the island, the day after Dagmar left the atelier. His last conversation with the young woman, in particular her reading of his mother's letter, had set him thinking. Then that morning the local newspaper reported the bones found on the islet off Hvar had been removed to Split for forensic tests. Tilde's remains were boxed up in some lab, unmourned and unacknowledged, maybe a brown paper label attached to the lid declaring her one of the many "Unknowns" left in history's wake. Antun knew he had to find a way of organising her reburial. Memories came to him then, memories of that last, terrible ceremony, Branko cradling Tilde's tiny body before Antun prised his fingers loose and let her be put in the ground. The smell of decay masked by a heavy odour of wet soil and lavender. Branko's tears noisy and troubled. She'd been buried all wrong, even then. Antun should have made her a headstone that declared proudly who lay beneath it; his half-sister, Jakob Eschenasi's daughter and Branko's wife-to-be. This really was unfinished business and he must find a way of sorting it, before he was incapable – or dead.

He knew he would have to talk with the surviving members of the Ostojić family, before taking action. That was why Marko was taking him back to the island, for the first time since the end of the Second World War. He'd asked Marko to phone Mara Ostojić, Branko's eldest sister, and make the necessary arrangements. And here he was, back on a boat, the wind in his hair and the salty air stinging at his lips and eyes. Marko was a good sailor, if not quite in the league of The Frenchie, Antun's old friend. He recalled Mara's husband Drago playing Caliban in *The Tempest* all those years ago, a thin, dark man with a heavy brow and a wall eye. *I'll show thee the best springs: I'll pluck thee berries: I'll fish for thee; and get thee wood enough*. He might as well have been describing how Branko made love to Tilde.

They set sail as early as they could, to avoid the vicious heat of a day in late July. It was a good plan in Antun's opinion, if only because the island had always looked its best just after daybreak, in the minutes before the islanders cracked open their doors and spilled out into the narrow, stone-flagged streets. On arrival, Marko had arranged to borrow a wheelchair from a local hotel to transport Antun up to Mara's house, close to the Napoleonic fort. Six o'clock in the morning, but the noise of ciacadas lurking amongst the huge cacti, which sprouted in abundance all over the island, was already deafening. Marko had to push uphill, but he wasn't deterred. Antun could walk for short bursts, so they made a leisurely, good-natured progress to Mara's home. She lived with Drago and two of her sons and their children in the old family home, inherited from her parents after their deaths in the late 1950s.

The house was reached by following a circuitous route through the streets where the fishermen of the island lived. Antun glimpsed into an open doorway and saw a woman ironing, a child next to her playing the piano. Outside another house, an old woman gutted fish on a small table. Flies hovered above the guts in the shape of a large, black funnel. The men's route continued upwards, broken only by jutting stone steps, some housing lemons ripening in the sun, others, pots of dusty flowers. There were notices everywhere warning people not to drop cigarettes, because of the danger of fires in such oven-hot conditions. A nun fanned a child's face by an open church door; a man in vest and shorts trotted past with a crate of light yellow peppers balanced on his head. Iron gates led into tiny courtyards, some flanked by piles of old stones, others shaded by little balconies, nearly all of them dwarfed by the satellite dishes wedged against their ornamental railings.

As they neared Mara's house, Antun could feel his courage returning. So much had changed, so much had stayed the same. He remembered the house was painted yellow and that it had always been busy. The rooms had been lined with precious icons, some cheap coloured engravings in homemade frames, but each one decorated with precious symbols, a thread of ribbon from a christening robe; a lock of hair; a dried stalk of lavender; or a snip of fabric from a jacket. Marko pushed open the small wooden door: it was like stepping back into the past. The kitchen they entered was full of life. Three boys were squabbling at the table over a kitten with too large a head which was trying to gobble up some spilled sugar. Drago was whetting knives and Mara was sweeping round the children and the kitten with a little broom made out of twigs. Everyone stopped when Antun was wheeled into the room. The boys didn't know him but were intrigued by his cloak. Marko oversaw the introductions and his easy charm soon won over everyone.

Mara and Antun escaped the throng, moving into a rarely used room next door to the kitchen. Antun looked long and hard at Branko's sister. This was the woman who had brought him back to life after Tilde's death and all the horrors that had preceded it. He'd given himself up to his private visions and nightmares; sketched them out on the tiles of the atelier floor, before translating them to paintings which he had no wish to share with anyone, bar Mara who worked carefully round him like he was an unexploded bomb. When he started work on the painting of "The Deer Wedding", he'd seen the scene so vividly, he'd cried out in amazement and she'd dropped a plate. Was he mad, or possessed of a brilliant idea? He recalled painting, hour after long hour, until his sight had blurred into a mess of different colours. Then he'd resorted to using the tips of his fingers, smudging over the canvas and matching colours as best he could, because the pigments blurred against his bruised eyelids. It was Mara who had found him, lying on the floor one morning, a shivering wreck. He'd gone blind.

"Grief has robbed you of your senses," she'd diagnosed. She nursed him with her work-worn hands, meshed with scars made by her gutting blade. He remembered how she had massaged his eyes, coaxing his sight to return with the coarse pads of her fingers. "Branko is still alive," she said. "He's a fish and a beast, travelling under water or by land, whatever is needed. He's a warrior, just like his ancestors who fought the Turk and kept our world from ruin. And he says to tell you: you are his brother."

Except Branko had drowned, leading a maritime patrol off the Dalmatian coast; he'd sunk five fathoms deep, spinning away out of the world, his arms and limbs spread out like a starfish. Maybe he'd joined Jakob's bones at the bottom of the sea? Dear God, but the past was just one long, cruel and relentless memory. For a minute, Antun wished he hadn't come, nearly called out for Marko to come and rescue him. Mara stepped up close, so close he could see the large copper hoop earrings she'd always favoured glinting in a finger of sunlight creeping in at the window. "Is it time?" she asked.

He nodded. "Marko has many contacts with the government and the media. He says we'll be able to tell the story as we wish to tell it. Branko's name will not suffer."

Mara smiled. She had lost most of her teeth and her skin bore the thick creases of her eighty-six years. But her smile transformed her into the teasing, vociferous girl she had once been, the one who had blatantly provoked the Italian director Fuesli by sewing costumes based on those worn by the Partisan fighters, the very people he was determined on hounding down and killing. "This is not the first time you've been in this room, you know."

Antun frowned, because he hadn't immediately caught her meaning.

"Look around you. This was the room you were born in."

He looked round as instructed: a stone-flagged floor, a truckle bed leaning against the wall, some chairs and an old chest. Pots of lavender and herbs grew in old tins on the windowsill, which looked out onto a small, square courtyard. There were lemon trees growing along the far wall and a canopy of vines formed a roof overhead. Antun liked the thought of Elenora living here, amongst the scent of fresh lemons and lavender. It was far better than remembering what had happened to her at the end of her life, murdered without dignity or trial, in the notorious Jasenovac camp complex set up on the bank of the River Sava by the Ustaše government to destroy its enemies.

Well, well. This was where he had been born, although he hadn't ever been nursed by his mother, as her letters had revealed. Maybe that's why he had always kept the world at bay? He had been given away and he'd forgotten the woman who had grown him inside her; the woman who had breathed with him and moved with him for nine long months. That precious intimacy, broken up with no explanation, because he'd been too tiny to understand words, or gestures. Antun thought a baby might be like the kitten he'd just left in the kitchen, snuffling up the scents of what it needed: milk smell and a mother's skin smell. All his senses would have been muddled up and confused when the scents changed too quickly and he had been conjured out of the lemon house into the chaos of a city. He'd been living the life of an exile from his very first day.

Mara stretched out one of her scarred hands. She wiped his cheeks carefully with a small handkerchief she'd pulled out from the front of her dress. "I know it's right we do this now, Antun. I saw them bring Tilde off the island and it broke my heart all over again. The one thing Branko could do for her, and now it's undone."

"I'm going to Split to talk to the authorities. I'm going to ask for her body back. If I have the strength, I will carve her stone myself."

"And what about Branko?"

"It was an accident. A tragic accident. I have done an interview with Marko explaining everything Branko told me on that dreadful night. And guess what? My plan is to exhibit Tilde's portrait, but with a new title. It will be called: "Portrait of his sister Tilde Eschenasi by Antun Fisković, 1940 – 1941"."

Mara clapped her hands and wiped her own tears away. "Do you remember when she dressed up in my clothes, Antun? Such a slip of a girl. She was completely lost in my smelly oilskin apron. And putting on my clogs must have been like wearing buckets on her feet."

Tilde had also worn Mara's panel skirt and favourite wool stockings. She'd held a clutch of fish on a piece of twine, and across her back, Mara's wicker basket used to transport fish to Split market. The fish had quickly gone off and she'd fainted more than once from the stench. "She suffered for my art, it's true," Antun admitted.

They re-joined the rest of Mara's family for an early lunch, and conversation had turned to the new production of *The Tempest* being rehearsed that week on the island's beach. "Madness, complete madness," Drago declared, spearing his grilled sardine on his fork and waving it at Antun. Drago had lent Branko and Antun his boat when they had decided to bury Tilde's body, away from Hvar. It had been Drago's idea that Antun use Fuesli as an ally. "He likes you, Antun. You're a fellow artist. See if he can find a way to stop the naval patrols for a while and let us do our job undisturbed." Antun had done more than that. He'd let Fuesli believe they were lovers; he'd encouraged his God awful poetry and let him fuck him in his studio. Antun and Branko had buried Tilde without trouble, but he'd earned himself the reputation of being an Ustaša. A reputation like that stuck like a burr; a reputation that had been used against idealists like Goran Petrić to such ugly effect. Antun remembered how Fuesli had paraded him around the harbourside at Split like a pet poodle, quoting at every opportunity his idol Mussolini: "Violence is profoundly moral, more moral than compromises and transactions." And yet there had been times when Antun wondered whether or not this man had been right in holding such an opinion. Hadn't he resorted to transactions that had merely compromised him still further in the eyes of many of his neighbours?

Marko had worked hard to calm him down when they finally arrived back at the atelier, later that same evening. The retrospective was going to set the record straight and dismiss once and for all the many confusions surrounding Antun's life.

"And all this is possible with a bunch of paintings and drawings?" Antun scoffed, but waited anxiously for Marko's dismissal of such pessimism.

"Croatia needs her stories to be told – and her own artists to tell them. You are the right man, living at the right time."

And what stories, Antun reflected, as he made his way to bed that night. Like that of the Partisan hero Branko Ostojić, who had been his friend from childhood. Branko had fought the Ustaše regime, convinced the Partisan leader Tito would, on victory, honour the islands with the status they had long been denied. He had no idea that Communism would impose its own set of political compromises on his country and its island communities. Antun barely recognised the history books' eulogies about his friend, who could, allegedly, wrestle a bear to the ground, or slit someone's throat without them even being aware of it. No mention ever of his secret love for Antun's half-sister, or how it ended in shambolic, terrible fashion on the night of a Partisan raid in Split. Under cover of that raid, Tilde had gone to meet Branko up at the chapel on Marjan Hill. They managed to avoid being seen by the military patrols in the city, but had argued over Branko's wish for Tilde to convert to Catholicism. She'd run away, fallen en route and smashed open her skull. Branko had followed and found her body. He'd carried her down to Antun's atelier, weeping silently and cowering in doorways as bullets were fired overhead in a street battle being fought between the Partisans and the Italian military.

Later, under cover of darkness, they'd buried Tilde on the islet where she had hoped to live with Branko in a restored shepherd's hut. Antun had improvised prayers round the grave as he helped Branko dig with shovels and their bare hands. Branko had worn his grief for his young lover's death like an iron coat. On their return to Split, Antun had watched his friend beat a retreat through its labyrinthe streets and it was as if he had been transported back centuries. How many other men had made their escape in just such a way, moving from one shadow to another with the quick, barely perceived motion of a firefly, their whole world carried on their backs and deep inside their hearts? Could history ever be stopped in its tracks to free people so that they could live across the cruel and arbitrary divides of religion, or social caste?

Sick and tormented as he was in the dying days of 1942, Mara had urged Antun to get strong again. "There are many who rely on you, did you but know it." She had him back on his feet by the New Year. She'd sat on the stool in front of him and bared her blackened teeth. "Go on, Mr Artist, paint me, if you dare." And Antun had laughed spontaneously for the first time in what felt like the whole of his life. Snow flakes the size of coins battened the shutters in his studio and the fire had spluttered in a heavy draught. Out of the corner of his eye, he'd seen the deer gather, picking their way daintily through a blanket of snow which reflected the sheen of their perfect white coats. And he'd understood then that his vision *was* a living thing, but it would be a long while before time was on his side and he could make others believe in it too.

Chapter 23
bard on the beach
Hvar, July 1998

The dress rehearsal of *The Tempest* is scheduled to start later this evening, but Zdenka and Dagmar have agreed to meet me beforehand to hear my news. My daughter sits cross-legged on a bench; Zdenka sits on the table in front of her, smoking at a leisurely pace. They turn heads even in the crowded piazza. Dagmar waves when she sees me. Zdenka is less welcoming, but I sense she's worried about the play as much as anything else, because she keeps taking calls on her mobile from the play's director. I order champagne, because I feel like celebrating, even though I haven't yet told them about my offer. It's a celebration already, because my daughter seems genuinely pleased to see me.

"You should have rung and let me know you were coming," she insists.

"I wasn't sure of my welcome."

Dagmar looks upset, so I quickly cover up my mistake. "I mean, you've both been so busy."

Zdenka lights up another cigarette and cuts straight to the point. "What's the big secret? Has the President offered you a job for old times' sake?"

Dagmar glares at her cousin, but she ignores her.

I explain what I've already said to Darko, that I want to help them fund their studies with money I have saved after the buy-out of *Neu Style* by a German publisher. "I'm not rich, but I can help you both. What do you say?"

Neither Zdenka or Dagmar speaks. They look at each other and then at their feet.

"You'll need time to think about it, I know. But please understand why I'm doing this. I just think you should have the opportunities that Goran and I fought so hard to win for ourselves."

Dagmar is the first to reply. She leans forward, fixing me with her green cat's eyes. "Ana, it's a fantastic offer. But I don't know if I want to study right now. So much has happened since I came here."

"The money can be used for whatever you want," I tell her. "No strings, really."

Zdenka coughs and puts out her cigarette. I've wrong footed her with my offer, I know. She's wearing a thin slip dress, its hem embroidered with little coloured stones. She fiddles with one of them rather than looking at me when she speaks. "How long do we have to think about this?"

"Well, there's no deadline. I want you to make the best decision in the time it takes, that's all."

Zdenka slides off the edge of the table and picks up her handbag. "It's too generous," she mutters, and heads off towards the beach.

I turn and look at Dagmar. She shrugs. "Zdenka is proud. It's a big thing for her to accept, you know that."

"Yes, I do. But I still hope she takes up my offer."

Dagmar checks her watch. It's time for her to go, but before leaving, she invites me to watch the rehearsal. We walk down to the beach and I take my place on the harbour wall. Further along, close to Hotel Lučić, the director Eos Parry-Jones parades the perimeter of the beach armed with clipboard and a maglite torch. A heavy beat issues from the Napoleonic fort, carried on the soft evening air. Dagmar has already explained it's not a conventional interpretation of Shakespeare's play but a loose adaptation made up of a series of tableaux. The first tableau suggests the power struggle at the heart of Prospero's banishment to the island. Various members of the cast hurl themselves mid-air, only to be caught as they land by their partner. It's aerial wrestling and very impressive to watch. Dagmar plays Miranda, an innocent child who accompanies her mother Prospera on her mission to persuade her father to let her return to Milan. A child-woman who must soon be wed to another Royal, but there aren't many of them living on an island. Dagmar moves in slow motion across the beach. She looks extraordinary, caught in the light of the theatre lanterns.

Eos calls out to Trinculo to start throwing the bottles that signal the arrival of the debauched ship crew. The air is so warm, I feel I could bathe in it. Trinculo starts a reel, quickly taken up by the whole company. A huge burst of acapello singing, drawing on a Ukrainian drinking song Eos has taught everyone. I notice some of the club crowd on the way to the fort have stopped to watch. Zdenka joins me briefly, pointing out how the director wants the play to develop like a series of freeze-frames in a film. "They mustn't stop acting for a second. Even when they're not in the tableaux, their characters must be kept busy." I spot Dagmar struggling to put on her bridal veil, a long fishing net attached to a coronet of big crystal flowers. She wears an amazing blue dress. I can't be sure, but I think it might be a Fortuny. Zdenka confirms my suspicions. "It's a present from Antun Fisković. His mother wore it, apparently."

She's away to deal with some faulty lantern and I'm left to watch as my daughter prepares for her beach wedding with a young drama student called Erik, a twig of an adolescent dressed in a pair of loose, dark blue Thai trousers. The music is haunting, reminiscent of Goran Bregović's music, thrilling chords played in counterpoint by a violinist and accordionist. Then Dagmar's friend Milica starts to sing and I'm struck by the supernatural quality of her voice. Passers by stop in their tracks, some sit down beside me. "Who is she?" they ask. I find myself turning show promoter, handing out leaflets Zdenka has left with me. "Tonight, just after one. Come and see the show and find out for yourselves."

But I have another task to complete before I can join the audience. I text Dagmar and ask her to meet me after rehearsal in the Mayor's restaurant, close to the Franciscan monastery. We order brodetto and pasticada and then I start to tell her what I really know about her father's investigation into Fisković's life. Some of it she's already pieced together, because she's managed to speak to the man himself. But there are some things Fisković has stayed silent on, namely the identity of the sitter for his famous portrait, his own half-sister.

"I don't understand," Dagmar interrupts me. "Why would he keep that quiet?"

"You must remember that Branko Ostojić was a famous war hero. It wouldn't have gone down well for him to be implicated in the death of a young woman, let alone a Jewess. The rumour Goran heard was that Ostojić killed Tilde, and Fisković helped cover the crime up. He did it by calling on help from his Ustaša lover, a translator called Fuesli. He worked for Italian intelligence."

"He did mention Fuesli. Was he blackmailing him?"

"Who knows, but it was possible. You see, Fisković was heavily compromised dealing with one of the island's occupiers and a committed Fascist. Imagine how that story sounded, thirty or so years ago, enemies circling your father like wolves, claiming he was one of the agitators intent on setting up a new Fascist state. And the shame it would have bought on the Ostojić family too. He was warned off. Goran never told me by whom, but I guessed word came from Belgrade, probably from one of Tito's longterm cronies."

"But the Ostojićs helped Fisković after the war. That doesn't suggest they though he was a killer."

"No. They knew the truth, because they knew about Elenora and Jakob. But others heard the story and at that time people used what they could for any cheap advantage. Besides which, Fisković was deeply reluctant to have his sexuality made public. All the lies and the misunderstandings that stemmed from that one fact. Goran knew about his male lovers. They went drinking together and he talked off the record. Goran even said there were rumours that Branko and Fisković were lovers, but I don't think that was true. He told Goran he wanted his childhood friend to marry his half-sister, that he made every effort to help them even when the Ustaše banned marriages between Croats and Jews."

Dagmar finishes her plate of brodeto and chews thoughtfully on a chunk of bread. "Lies are such dangerous, stupid things, aren't they? I mean, all those lies told about Tilde over the years. Her love affair and her death hushed up it's like it never happened. That's so tragic." My daughter pauses. Something else is snagging at her thoughts, not just a tragic love affair from the past. "Ana, I've met someone here on the island. He's a fisherman. And a student too."

I'm startled at first, but then delighted. My daughter has just confided her own secret to me. It feels like a corner has been turned.

"He's at university in Siena."

"Is this why you can't make up your mind about art college?"

Dagmar smiles. "I just don't know what's going to happen after the show and everything. Maybe I'll go to Italy too. I don't know yet."

She tells me more about Kristijan, who she hopes to introduce me to at the after show party. She also explains how much it meant coming to the island and to Split, to follow in her father's footsteps and to come to a clearer understanding of what happened to him. "He was ill, wasn't he? And he was put under such terrible pressure. You both were. It wasn't personal, what he did, was it?"

"No, it wasn't. And you know something, when we first talked and I got so cross with you for looking into Goran's past, well, it was because I recognised something I thought I had forgotten. Goran was just as stubborn as you are. Find a reason not to do something, and he would find a dozen more to contradict me. Like father, like daughter."

"Really?"

Dagmar's face lights up, like a bright winter sun.

"Yes, really. You are your father's daughter."

Chapter 24
sea wedding
Hvar, July 1998

Walking down to the beach, I try and rehearse each cue and line and discover I can't remember anything. I'm a bag of nerves by the time I reach my spot on the beach, lit up by a lantern. Eos is close by, in a conversation with the dressmaker. My bridal veil has been further embellished with stones, shells and other bits of bric a brac. It's heavy when I pull it up to fix the coronet on my head. Eos orders me to keep my back straight; the dressmaker darts around sticking pins here and there. The finishing touches are done as the tide flows out.

My hands shook so much when I first picked up the veil, Milica spontaneously hugged me. That gesture surprised us both. Now, with the veil stored away for later, my friend and I hold hands and wait for the show to begin. At precisely two o'clock in the morning, an acapello harmony rings out from across the water and I see Kristijan towing his boat from the far end of the promenade, towards our al fresco stage. Six of the company stand inside the boat, singing a song that Milica has written about a storm. We bang the boat's sides with our sticks and then jump into the water. Running and screaming and calling out our character's key words, which have been whispered to us by Eos during rehearsals. *Heart. Rememberance. Paragon. Desire. Brave.* These are all my words. I throw them out, any which way, and jump into the Movement Director Andrej's waiting arms. He spins me over his head and pulls me back down, guiding me to the beach with tapered fingers curled against my spine. The shipwreck is proceded by duets between earth creatures and sprites, accompanied by an accordion, a violin and a cello. It's still very hot, even working by moonlight. Milica starts singing and the atmosphere turns more wonderful still. I have no idea what the audience on the harbour side makes of this, but I'm burning up with adrenaline.

My wedding is a stately procession, all the way from the lanterns lining the harbour wall to the edge of the water. I change behind the banana tree into my cornflower blue dress. Ferdinand places the coronet on my head and a group of sprites arrange the folds of the fishing net around me, in the shape of a large open fan. Slowly, I walk out into the sea with my husband, the lanterns now all turned to illuminate our disappearing backs. We walk in dazzling light, made more wonderful still by a retinue of jumping, silver-backed fish. Kristijan waits in the fishing boat before plucking me up and carrying me away. I barely hear the riot of applause as the show finishes. I'm wrapped in a wet fishing net, lying at the bottom of a boat. I look up at the moon and it's a perfect disc of silvery loveliness. My face is its mirror; I feel liquid brilliant, just like the silver flecked water beneath deck.

Back on shore, Fisković is among several guests waiting for me in the terrace bar. I've changed into the mini crochet dress Zdenka bought for me in Zagreb. In the bar, my mother Ana is deep in conversation with Marko Strgar. I join Fisković, who sits close by. He wears an old leather jacket and black jeans. For a minute, I don't recognise him because I'm so used to seeing him in his glittering cloak. He's enjoyed the show, and picked up on a great deal. "Your mother and Marko acted as my eyes, so I didn't miss a thing," he explains.

Returning to the island has made him reflective. Marko has already told him that Ana has revealed Tilde's sad history to me. He has been quick (as ever) to get the details he needs to keep one step ahead of us all. Fisković now tells me that Tilde's eyes are included in his painting "The Deer Wedding".

"The eyes of the first deer in the line; then Branko's eyes, my eyes and last of all your eyes." He pauses and takes a few sips of his Jamnica water. "I knew I couldn't keep silent about Tilde any longer," he continues. "Not after she was taken back on shore. The idea of her remains lying in a box somewhere, unmourned. It was impossible. I've been to the authorities in Split today and I've told them what I know. There will be no charges."

"And the Ostojićs?"

I remember the little old lady falling to the ground when the news of the body found on the island spread like wildfire, just after my arrival. That woman was Mara Ostojić, Antun reveals, Branko's eldest sister. "We have kept our secret together," he says. Mara's grief was compounded by having to keep quiet about the truth of Antun's birthright. Mara, like Antun, had been worried that Branko might get to know too much and that would have put many other lives at risk, if he had been arrested by the Ustaše. My euphoria filters away as Antun continues his story. He understands my change in mood and smiles reassurance. "I have also arranged for Tilde to be buried in the Jewish Cemetery in Split. I'm putting money from any exhibition sales into a restoration fund for the site. You see, my half-sister was first and foremost a Jew. She took pride in that fact. She will be buried next to her mother Hepzibah. And I shall also make a memorial for my father Jakob, if it is the last thing I ever do." He holds up frail arms, but the hands still look strong and hardy. "Marko will help me find the stone and he will devise exercises to keep my fingers working."

It's a good plan and I salute Antun with a glass of champagne. A small breeze builds up as we sit drinking in a new morning. In a few days time, I will have to leave Hvar.

"You will come back to us, won't you?" Antun's hands fold round mine, and he stares at me with his filmy eyes. "The island has won you over too, hasn't it?"

I cannot disagree. Zdenka is less enamoured of the island, but that's because Anthony is waiting for her back in Zagreb. She confesses at the terrace party that he has proposed and she has accepted. Dear God, my wicked cousin getting married!

"Don't take the piss," she warns. "We're perfect for each other. Even Aunty Rozana has forgiven him, because he bought her a new Jesus for the guest toilet."

"Zdenka!"

"No, really he did. Chose it all by himself. We'll make a Catholic of him yet."

She waltzes away with Marko, but she's just playing with him whilst she has time; each spin in her towering, petrol blue heels is really bringing her closer and closer to her United Nations hero. We are all spiralling away into a future that will never have to endure the terrible secrets of past generations. We are stepping out in wide-eyed awe, like Miranda in her sea wedding. And somewhere, close by, I really do believe that four white deer have walked through a forest, safeguarding our future with a union completed in a timeless, magical silence.

My mother reveals she'd once dismissed the story as "nothing but some silly nonsense of your father's". But in truth, she'd always been delighted by her unusual birthday gift, which Goran had asked Fisković to write down for her. She still carries the story in her purse. After dancing with both Zdenka and my mother, Marko comes and joins Fisković and myself. He reveals that "The Deer Wedding" will form the centrepiece in the retrospective opening at Mimara next year. "Your mother is delighted," he says, glancing over at her. "She's very keen to write about the exhibition in her magazine. We've discussed several ideas tonight, already."

Towards dawn, Fisković pleads tiredness and Marko prepares to take him back to the mainland. Milica and I end up sleeping on the beach, long after our other party guests have headed back to their various destinations. Milica has slept outside many times in the past, but this time she does it from choice and because she's so excited by all that happened this evening. She thinks the terrace bar might give her work next summer as a musician to entertain diners. We plot our futures, staring up at an indigo night sky, still thick with stars. Another line from Shakespeare's play comes back to me on the verge of sleep. It was a line I had recited under my breath, as I watched Kristijan cut through the water earlier this evening, his shoulders like two, curved scimitar blades caught in starlight: *Then to the elements / Be free and fare thou well...*

Centuries lie between the day Shakespeare wrote that line and the evening I whispered it under my breath; hours, weeks, months and years that have folded into each other like falling leaves. And yet the past feels as close to me as the silk skin of my Fortuny dress; the future is closer still, as close as Kristijan, walking through a shoal of jumping silver fish. A twist of his star-lit shoulders and his head turned, long enough for his eyes to find mine inside the depths of the shadows tracing our temporary island stage.

On research and inspiration

This novel focuses on events in two specific periods of Croatian history: 1941 and the setting up of the first Independent State of Croatia, and the late 1990s, when a second attempt at independence was forged, following the Yugoslav war of 1991 – 1995.

I travelled to Croatia in 1998, nearly three years after the war ended. Hostilities were growing on the border in Kosovo and earlier that same year there had been a run on the main banks in the country, which had collapsed, causing economic turmoil. There had been a small recovery in the number of tourists visiting the Dalmatian coast, but that was affected again the following year with the situation in Kosovo deteriorating still further and the death of Croatia's President Tudman. This was a country still emerging from war; the UN had personnel monitoring various parts of the country and there were many displaced people living in hotels on the islands and on the mainland in Split.

I was a journalist at the time, and had received funding from British Council Zagreb to write about the forging of links between a young Croatia and small nations such as Wales. What particularly interested me was writing about a place where history is still a living (and unspent) force, and, inevitably, the question of whether it is possible to trace out a future when so much has been broken and destroyed. The characters in the novel are entirely figments of my imagination. However, reference is made to a number of historical figures. The following notes provide context for some of the events in which these people feature. Whilst the artwork created by Antun Petrić does not exist, it is possible to view "Stag's Wedding" by Ivan Generalić in the Croatian Museum of Naïve Art in Zagreb.

Aleksandar, King of Yugoslavia. In 1929, the King proclaimed a royal dictatorship. Political parties were abolished and the Kingdom of Serbs, Croats and Slovenes renamed the Kingdom of Yugoslavia. Many Croats calling for greater autonomy were arrested.

Ante Pavelić. In November 1929, Pavelić was sentenced to death in absentia for publicly advocating the overthrow of the state. He fled to

Mussolini's Italy where he set up training camps for the organisation he had founded, the Ustaše Croatian Revolutionary Organisation. In October 1934, Pavelić was involved in the assassination of King Aleksandar on a state visit to France. He was imprisoned in Italy, but later released. In April 1941, he returned to Zagreb, with Mussolini's support, and became leader (Poglavnik) of the Independent State of Croatia.

Croatia was in effect split between Germany and Italy during the war; the Italian "sphere of influence" ran from North Dalmatia down to Split. Germany's "sphere of influence" included Zagreb, Slavonia and North Bosnia. When Germany surrendered in 1945, Pavelić managed to evade capture by Tito's victorious Partisans. He died in Spain in 1957.

Milan Stojadinović. Served as Yugoslav Prime Minster from 1935 – 38. His government actively sought the favour of the Fascist powers of Italy and Germany.

Josip Broz "Tito". Tito was leader of the Yugoslav Communist Party. By 1943, Tito's Partisans were in control of the former Italian–occupied zone of Dalmatia. In 1944, Tito entered Belgrade with the support of Russia's Red Army. In November 1945, the Yugoslav monarchy was abolished and Yugoslavia declared a People's Republic.

Franjo Tudman. Tudman became President of the newly created Croatian Democratic Union in February 1989. A Croat Partisan, his disillusion with Yugoslav Communism later turned into an expression of more extreme nationalist dissident views. In June 1991, Croatia was declared a "sovereign and independent state" but it was against a background of increasing violence. By 1993, Croat-on- Muslim fighting in Bosnia was causing international concern, including incidents such as the demolition of Mostar's famous medieval bridge. Tudman's presidency was challenged in October 1993 by an open letter from a group of Croat intellectuals calling on him to resign.

Guide to Pronunciation

Serbo-Croat and its respective languages are pronounced phonetically.

A a as in father
B b as in bath
C ts as in its
Č ch as in cheese (hard ch)
Ć ch as in future (soft ch)
D d as in down
Đ j as in jeans (soft j)
Dž dj as in adjust (hard dj)
E e as in met
F f as in five
G g as in grand
H h as in hat
I ee as in feet
J y as in yellow
K k as in kick
L l as in love
Lj li as in billion
M m as in more
N n as in need
Nj ni as in onion
O o as in or
P p as in put
R r as in raw (rolled r)
S s as in sweet
Š sh as in shape
T t as in top
U oo as in loop
V v as in victory
Z z as in zebra
Ž s as in pleasure

Acknowledgements

A huge thank you to Firenza Guidi, artistic director of ELAN, who invited me to join her team for *In the Name of the Body*, a remarkable production staged on a beach on Hvar island in 1998. That experience inspired many aspects of my fictional version of events. Thank you also to Ian Fordham at Broad Bay House, Isle of Lewis, for providing a place of inspiration and amazing hospitality. Rounds of applause for David (Digi) and Anna Massey of Goldlion; DJ Evans; British Council Zagreb; Kristijan C; Mark Bristow; Michael Symmons Roberts; the Ivan Meštrović Gallery and Kaštelet in Split, Croatia, and last, but not least, my editor Gwen Davies for her judicious editing. I'm also indebted to Rebecca West's *Black Lamb and Grey Falcon* (Penguin Classics), Marcus Tanner's *Croatia, A Nation Forged in War* (Yale University Press), Robert D Kaplan's *Balkan Ghosts, A Journey Through History* (Picador) and Shakespeare's *The Tempest* (Penguin Popular Classics). Special thanks for to Danijela Spirić for her advice on the Serbo-Croat language and for proofreading my manuscript.

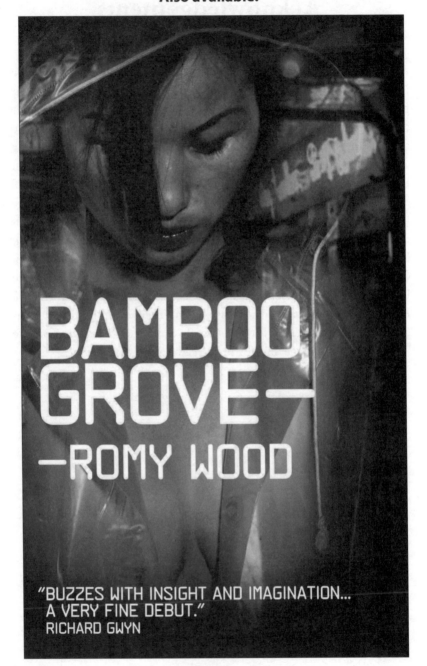

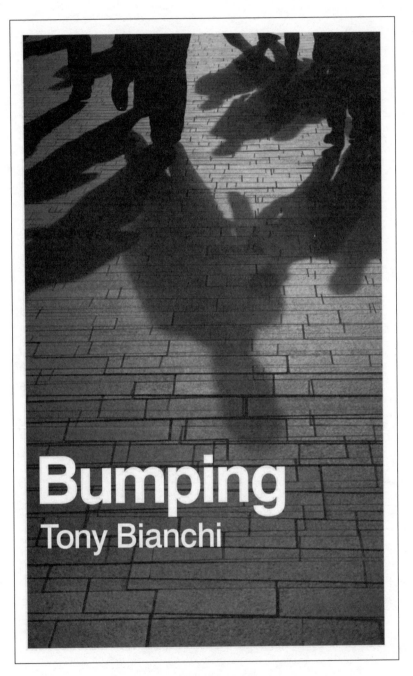

£9.99

ALCEMI

www.alcemi.eu

TALYBONT CEREDIGION CYMRU SY24 5HE
e-mail gwen@ylolfa.com
phone (01970) 832 304
fax 832 782